CLASSIC
FILM
SCRIPTS

Film   Green, Graham
PN
1997   The Third man
G694
1988
808.82 Gre

D0879019

THE THIRD MAN

a film by

Graham Greene
and Carol Reed

Lorrimer Publishing

WATKINS INSTITUTE
LIBRARY

771.1
G799

All rights reserved including the right
of reproduction in whole or in part in any form
This edition copyright © 1968 by Graham Greene
Published by Lorrimer Publishing Incorporated
First printing 1973
Revised edition 1984
Publisher and Editor: Andrew Sinclair

Greene, Graham
　The third man.
　I. Title
　791.43'72　　　　PN1997

　ISBN 0-85647-093-7

Distributed exclusively in the United States of America,
its territories, possessions, protectorates, mandated territories,
the Philippines and Canada by Frederick
Ungar Publishing Company Incorporated,
36 Cooper Square, New York, N.Y. 10003

This book is sold subject to the condition that it shall not,
by way of trade or otherwise, be lent, re-sold, hired out,
or otherwise circulated without the publisher's prior consent
in any form of binding or cover other than that in which it is
published and without a similar condition including this condition
being imposed on the subsequent purchaser

Distributed exclusively in the United Kingdom and
Commonwealth by Lorrimer (Sales) Limited.

Inquiries should be addressed to Lorrimer Publishing Limited,
16 Tite Street, London SW3 4HZ.

Cover design: Fred Price

44232
WATKINS INSTITUTE
LIBRARY

CONTENTS

ACKNOWLEDGEMENTS

We wish to thank Carol Reed, who was kind enough to lend his personal copy of the script, and Graham Greene, who personally vetted it before publication.

We also wish to thank Martin Hayden for his assistance in the preparation of this book. Our thanks are also due to Joel Finler, the British Film Institute and the Museum of Modern Art, New York, for the use of their stills.

INTRODUCTION

The Third Man called on the genius of an extraordinary quartet: Graham Greene and Carol Reed and Orson Welles and Alexander Korda. It set a particular style for British films, a combination of realism of background and penetration of character, based on the two main qualities of the British wartime cinema, a feeling for documentary detail and social purpose. Carol Reed explained the success of the film, shot in 1949, by saying that it was one of the first British films allowed to be made chiefly on location. Until that time, making films in studios had falsified and glamourised all. In this film, the wet, brooding labyrinths of ruined and occupied Vienna express the traps and ambiguities facing people there, the harsh and shifting choices forced on the survivors of the war. Men plot out their little schemes in front of an arras of urban disaster. Harry Lime scuttling across the bomb-sites, the small operator trying to get rich on the surface of a total waste, is the symbol of the futility of shrewdness in the face of devastation. Lime tries to exploit war and shortages; he dilutes the life-giving penicillin until it gives death. But he is caught in the same vicious circle and in a closed city; as the British Military Policeman Calloway says, "A rat would have more chance in a closed room without a hole and a pack of terriers loose". War and its aftermath crushes all individuals, however clever they may be.

Originally, Korda sent Greene to Vienna to find a contemporary story there, which Greene grafted onto an old idea about meeting a dead man called Harry. He began by writing the screenplay as a story. "One cannot make the first act of creation in script form," he declared, "one must have the sense of more material than one needs to draw on." After writing the story, he worked closely with Reed on the script, which Reed changed in the shooting and editing of the film.

Because of Greene's reputation and the interest of this creative process, the script of *The Third Man* has been printed in full. Notes and brackets show the additions and omissions made by Carol Reed, and even Orson Welles, in the final version of the film. The script serves as a model lesson of how even the most brilliant and detailed of screenplays has to be changed in the process of making a film.

Most of the changes were for the purpose of clarifying the action or of setting the location, for *The Third Man* is the epitome of the well-made film. Other changes had to do with the problems of casting; the parts of Tombs and Carter were originally written for the comedy pair of Basil Radford and Naunton Wayne, but their dialogue had to be scrambled together when Wilfred Hyde White was cast to play both the parts as one man, Crabbit. Other changes had to do with the suggestions of the stars; Orson Welles's famous speech on the Swiss cuckoo clock, as he leaves the Great Wheel, was very much his own inspiration. Some written action was simply not translatable in terms of the cinema, or better done another way on the spot. Some small changes crept in for the sake of improvement or plausibility: Rollo Martins became Holly Martins, Anna came from Czechoslovakia, Tyler was replaced by a suave Rumanian called Popescu. The world-famous shots of the hands of the zither-player, Anton Karas, playing the 'Harry Lime' theme, came from Carol Reed's chance use of a local café, where Karas played for tips. Above all, the opening of the film had to be shot three months after the main shooting was officially completed, because the producer found that the location and situation were insufficiently explained for a mass audience. Carol Reed himself narrated the opening.

Such are the changes and compromises that lie between a screenplay and a film. Yet all in all, the film of *The Third Man* shows devotion by the director to the script. Carol Reed was kind enough to lend his personal copy of the script for printing, and Graham Greene personally vetted it before publication, for he has wisely retained all literary rights in the property (a rare and usually impossible thing to do). Orson Welles gives his finest acting performance outside *Citizen Kane*. And the result is a classic film, which does not date, but sets down for ever the horror and trickery and chaos of human lives in the sad mess left at the war's end.

ANDREW SINCLAIR

MAIN CHARACTERS

ROLLO (HOLLY) MARTINS:

A Canadian, aged about 35. He has been invited to Vienna by his old friend, Harry Lime, to write propaganda for a volunteer medical unit Lime runs. A simple man who likes his drink and his girl, with more courage than discretion. He has a great sense of loyalty towards Lime whom he met first at school, and even his blunderings are conditioned by his loyalty.

His love for Anna arises from the fact that she shares his devotion to Lime. Unlike Lime he has never made much out of life. He is an unsuccessful writer of Westerns, who has never seen a cowboy, and he has no illusions about his own writing.

HARRY LIME:

Harry Lime has always found it possible to use his devoted friend. A light, amusing, ruthless character, he has always been able to find superficial excuses for his own behaviour. With wit and courage and immense geniality, he has inspired devotion both in Rollo Martins and the girl Anna, but he has never felt affection for anybody but himself. He has run his medical unit to help his racket in diluted penicillin.

ANNA SCHMIDT:

An Estonian (Czechoslovakian), and therefore officially a Russian citizen, she has been living in Vienna and working as a small part actress under the protection of forged Austrian papers procured for her by Harry Lime, whom she loves. Unlike Martins she has few illusions about Harry. She has loved him for what he is and not for what she has imagined him to be, and his death leaves her completely indifferent as to her own fate.

Col. CALLOWAY:

In charge of the British Military Police in Vienna. A man with a background of Scotland Yard training; steady, patient and determined in his work — a man who is always kindly up to the point when it interferes with the job, who never gets angry (because it would be unprofessional) and regards Martins with amused tolerance.

Sgt. PAINE:

An ex-London policeman whose spiritual home is the Tottenham Court Road and the streets around it. He has the same professional calm and patience as his Colonel, for they are both, as it were, from the same school — London and the Yard, the charge room and the Courts — He is the only man in Vienna who knows Martins's books, and he admires them greatly.

Capt. CARTER (CRABBIT):

With his companion, Tombs, Carter has been shifted from regimental duties (for the good of the regiment) to the Cultural Re-education Section of G.H.Q. He is glad to be out of uniform (it enables him to eat in Austrian restaurants), and the only shadow on the new easy life of organising lectures, etc., at the Cultural Institute is the fear that some mistake may put him back in uniform again. In spite of this fear he is an ebullient, optimistic character.

Capt. TOMBS (CRABBIT):

Unlike Carter, Tombs is saturnine. He has little hope that this culture racket will last. Needless to say that neither man has any idea of how the new job should be done, nor indeed of the meaning of culture.

Dr. WINKEL:

Harry Lime's doctor and confederate. Very precise, very neat, very clean and unforthcoming. A collector of religious *objets d'art* without any belief in religion.

Baron KURTZ:

Harry Lime's chief confederate. An aristocrat who has come down in the world and now plays a violin at the Casanova night club. He manages to keep a certain faded elegance and charm, but like his *toupée* it doesn't quite ring true.

TYLER (POPESCU):

An American attached to an American cultural mission in Vienna, who has been enlisted by Lime, apparently very trustworthy, with tousled grey hair and kindly long-sighted humanitarian eyes; one would have said a really good American type.

JOSEPH HARBIN:

A medical orderly at a military hospital who first acted as an agent for Lime in obtaining penicillin, but later became an informer used by the police to procure information against the racketeers. He has disappeared when the story opens.

PORTER:

An elderly man employed in the block where Lime lived; a cautious, nervous man who does not want to get involved in anything. He has heard the accident which so conveniently disposed of Lime and saw the body carried by three men. As only two men gave evidence at the inquest, his evidence would have been of great value, but he did not come forward.

CREDITS

Production	Alexander Korda/David O. Selznick/London Films
Produced and directed by	Carol Reed
Original story and screenplay by	Graham Greene
Music by	Anton Karas
Associate producer	Hugh Perceval
Production Manager	T. S. Lyndon-Haynes
Art Director	Vincent Korda
Assistant art directors	John Hawkesworth and Joseph Bato
Director of Photography	Robert Krasker
Edited by	Oswald Hafenrichter
Camera Operators	Edward Scaife and Denys Coop
Additional photography by	John Wilcox and Stan Pavey
Sound	John Cox
Make-up	George Frost
Chief Hairdresser	Joe Shear
Wardrobe	Ivy Baker
Set dresser	Dario Simoni
Continuity	Peggy McClafferty
Zither music arranged and played by	Anton Karas
Length	9,428 ft.
Time	1 hour 44 minutes
Shot	At the London Film Studios, Shepperton, England, and on location in Austria

The Third Man won the Grand Prix for the best feature film in the 1949 International Film Festival at Cannes.

CAST

Holly Martins	Joseph Cotten
Anna	Alida Valli
Harry Lime	Orson Welles
Major Calloway	Trevor Howard
Sergeant Paine	Bernard Lee
Porter	Paul Hoerbiger
Porter's wife	Annie Rosar
' Baron ' Kurtz	Ernst Deutsch
Popescu	Siegfried Breuer
Dr. Winkel	Erich Ponto
Crabbit	Wilfrid Hyde-White
Anna's landlady	Hedwig Bleibtreu
Hansl	Herbert Halbik
Brodsky	Alexis Chesnakov
Hall porter at Sacher's	Paul Hardtmuth

NOTE

In our series of film scripts, we hope that The Third Man *will serve as a precise example of the change of a shooting script into a film. Square brackets denote the parts of the script Carol Reed was unable to film, for technical or other reasons. Footnotes show any important additions made to the script by the completed film. Perhaps the most important is the opening, so necessary to explain to the public the setting of the story. The beginning of the film is as follows:*

> *Credits roll out over a huge close-up of the strings of a zither. Sound of the ' Harry Lime ' theme playing.*
>
> *Many different shots of Vienna.*

VOICE *over* : I never knew the old Vienna before the war, with its Strauss music, its glamour and easy charm — Constantinople suited me better. I really got to know it in the classic period of the Black Market — *Shot of boots and stockings changing hands* — we'd run anything, if people wanted it enough and had the money to pay. Of course, a situation like that does tend to amateurs — *Shot of a body floating in an icy river* — but you know they can't stay the course like a professional. *Shot of a poster: ' YOU ARE NOW ENTERING THE AMERICAN ZONE '.* Now the city is divided into four zones, each occupied by a power — *Shots of British, Russian and French posters* — the Americans, the British, the Russians and the French. But the centre of the city — that's international, policed by an International Patrol. *Shot of guard duty being changed.* One member of each of the four powers. What a hope they had, all strangers to the place and none of them could speak the same language, except for a sort of smattering of German. *Shot of jeep-load of mixed guards, all silent.* Good fellows on the whole, even if it doesn't look any worse than a lot of other European cities, bombed about a bit . . . Oh wait, I was going to tell you — *Shots of bomb-sites* — I was going to tell you about Holly Martins from America — he came all the way here to visit a friend of his — *Shot of*

12

soldiers standing on parade in a square. The name was Lime, Harry Lime. *Soldiers are now seen marching.* Now Martins was broke and Lime had offered him — I don't know — some sort of a job. Anyway, there he was, poor chap, happy as a lark and without a cent. *Shot of a train pulling into the station. The theme music swells with the train pulling in.* HOLLY MARTINS *gets off the train and walks through the barrier, looking for someone.*

Guards from the four zones wait at the barrier.
AMERICAN GUARD : Passports please . . .
[*Continue as in the screenplay, see page 15*]

THE THIRD MAN

[1. INSERT CANADIAN PASSPORT (Before main title).
The passport is on a desk. A pair of hands opens it show-
ing the identification photograph with the name below
— ROLLO MARTINS. *Over scene we hear the faint clicking*
of a typewriter.

VICE CONSUL *voice only* : Remember, Vienna is an occupied
city. You must be extremely careful to observe all official
regulations.

MARTINS *voice only* : I know.

VICE CONSUL *voice only* : Just one more thing . . . whom are
you staying with in Vienna?

MARTINS *voice only* : With a friend of mine named Lime . . .
Harry Lime.

VICE CONSUL *voice only* : Address?

MARTINS *voice only* : 15 Stiftgasse.

One hand holds the passport while the other goes out of
frame a moment, brings in a stamp and presses it to the
opposite page of the passport picture. As it is lifted we
see the printed impression — it is a visa to the military
zone of Vienna.

ALLIED MILITARY PERMIT
VIENNA

The strains of a Strauss waltz swell up. The hand closes
the passport and holds it up. Another hand takes it,
camera pulls back to interior Canadian Passport office.
ROLLO MARTINS *is taking passport, says something in*
thanks to the official who has stamped it and turns to
go out of the office.

2. EXTERIOR AERODROME (DAY):
A Constellation is warming up, MARTINS *goes aboard,*
waving back off scene to someone very cheerfully.

3. CREDIT TITLES:
(*After each title card the following background scenes*

remain in the clear for a few feet, establishing the progress of MARTINS'S *journey.*)

1. MARTINS *in his seat looks round at his fellow passengers, then out of the window — settles down and opens a book.*
2. *Aerial shot of Constellation over the ocean.*
3. MARTINS *in his seat, eating from a tray. The plane dips suddenly, spilling a glass of tea into his lap.*
4. *Night, over the ocean. (The titles are now in white.)*
5. MARTINS, *dozing uneasily in his seat, wakes up, tries to find a comfortable position for his legs as he turns from one side to the other.*
6. *Dawn, and the plane coming in over Paris, with the Eiffel Tower in the background. (The titles are in black again.)*
7. *French Customs and Immigration Officials examining* MARTINS'S *passport and papers as he explains at length some story which we cannot hear.*
8. MARTINS *getting aboard another plane — a different plane this time.*
9. *Aerial shots crossing countryside which changes from fertile valleys to Swiss Alps.*
10. MARTINS *asleep in the plane weary and unshaven, getting progressively untidier and unhappier.*
11. MARTINS *feeling ill.*
12. *Another set of Customs and Immigration officials examining his passport and another explanation by* MARTINS; *this time he is very weary of the whole business.*
13. MARTINS *looking eagerly out of his plane window, bleary-eyed with a very unsightly stubble covering his face.*
14. *As the credits dissolve out we see Vienna in the clear. Then the word:*

VIENNA

As this dissolves out again:

4. ANIMATION (over the aerial shot)
Heavy black lines that show the various zones of the occupying powers. The names of the area are established

simultaneously: Russian — French — British — American. Hold on this long enough to establish the crazy patchwork that is Vienna today. MARTINS'S *plane swoops past camera and down towards the city.*

5. AIRPORT (DAY):

The passengers disembark from the plane and line up at the barrier where soldiers of the four powers, all in full uniform and armed, are examining their papers. All types are in the line — an American business man, a British officer, a young woman and her child, etc. MARTINS *is about fourth in line, carrying his passport in his hand and looks eagerly towards the barrier, as though searching for someone in the waiting throng at the other side. The passengers in front and behind him are waving to relatives and friends who have come to meet them, talking in all languages of the occupying forces, as well as German.* MARTINS *seems a little anxious as he reaches the soldiers of the four powers, not having spotted the person he is looking for. One of the soldiers takes his passport, glances at it and passes it to the other three in routine fashion.*]

BRITISH OFFICER [*to others:* Canadian — Martins.] *To* MARTINS, *as they glance over his papers*: What is the purpose of your visit, Mr. Martins?

MARTINS : I've been offered a job by a friend of mine . . .

BRITISH OFFICER : Where are you staying?

MARTINS : With him . . . Stiftgasse 15.

BRITISH OFFICER : His name?

MARTINS *has had to repeat this too many times.*

MARTINS : Lime — Harry Lime.

[*As the* OFFICER *makes a note of this,* MARTINS *looks towards barrier anxiously.*][1]

MARTINS : I thought he'd be here to meet me.

[*During this the men look at the papers, pass them around, glance somewhat strangely at* MARTINS, *then hand them back to the* BRITISH OFFICER, *who returns them to* MARTINS.

---

1 In the film, the OFFICER lets MARTINS through, and says ' Okay.'

BRITISH OFFICER *nods him on*: Right, Mr. Martins . . .

> MARTINS *stows his papers away and moves on, through the barrier. He looks around hopefully for a sign of his friend, watches as a man greets the woman with the baby, hugging and kissing her lovingly, then moves on towards a desk marked INFORMATION.*

MARTINS *to girl at desk*: Has anyone left a message for me? Martins — Rollo Martins . . .?

GIRL *glancing at her papers*: No, sir . . .

MARTINS: You sure? I'm expecting a friend — his name's Lime — he said he'd be here . . .

GIRL: I'm sorry . . .

> MARTINS *nods and crosses thoughtfully to the baggage section where the other passengers are busy claiming their bags.*

6. AIRPORT: LOCATION (DAY):

> *As* MARTINS *stands outside a crowded bus, his valise in hand, still looking around for his friend, the last passengers are aboard and the* DRIVER *starts up his motor, looking out at* MARTINS *warningly.*

DRIVER *in German*: We're leaving, sir . . . *In English*. We go now . . .

> MARTINS *turns and gets into the bus, taking a seat up front near the* DRIVER. *The bus pulls out of scene.*

7. TRAVELLING SHOTS: LOCATION (DAY):

> *As the bus makes its way through the ruined and devastated parts of Vienna, showing* MARTINS'S *reactions to the scenes, obviously new to him, for he looks with great interest and with a sense of revulsion.*

8. STREET: LOCATION (DAY):

> *As* MARTINS *gets out of the bus with his bag, the driver pointing down the street and saying something we cannot hear.* MARTINS *nods and starts off in the direction he has been shown. A ratty little* MAN *has been watching him surreptitiously. Now he falls in beside him, and in a whining manner, asks him something.* MARTINS *glances at him, then turns away, shaking his head in dismissal as he walks.*
>
> *The* MAN *continues to follow him, pleading.* MARTINS

gives him a cigarette. The man slouches away, satisfied]. MARTINS arrives at a flat and looks up at the entrance, comparing the address to the one on a paper in his hand. The address on the door reads 15 Stiftgasse. He hurries in.

9. 15 STIFTGASSE STAIRCASE: PART LOCATION (DAY):

MARTINS is making his way as rapidly as he can with his bag up the stairs. He rings the bell of HARRY LIME's flat which he can recognise on the third floor by the name plate, and opening the letter box, he whistles. While he waits, he examines such things as the hooks for brushing the clothes outside the doors and the spy holes to observe people. There is no reply to his ring and no answer comes. He rings a second and then a third time. Suddenly a voice speaks to him in German. The PORTER is standing two floors above.

PORTER: Es hat keinen Zweck so zu lauten, es ist niemand hier.

MARTINS: Huh? Speak English?

PORTER *in bad English, shouting to make himself understood*: You have just missed them.

MARTINS: Missed who?

PORTER: His friends and the coffin.

MARTINS looks up with surprise and apprehension.

MARTINS: Coffin?

PORTER: Mr. Lime's.

MARTINS stares at the PORTER who realises his mistake.

PORTER: Didn't you know? ... An accident ... run over by a car ... saw it myself ... on his own doorstep ... bang, bowled down like a rabbit. Killed at once. They'll have a difficult time burying him in this frost.

On the PORTER's voice and the look of distress on MARTINS's face, slowly dissolve.

10. CENTRAL CEMETERY: LOCATION (DAY):

MARTINS is looking about him — he speaks to an official who points down the huge snow-bound park. Avenues of graves, each avenue numbered and lettered stretching out like spokes of an enormous wheel. [On some grave-

*stones are the photographs of the occupants. Respectable
faces with waxed moustaches and morning coats. A huge
figure in armour on the family vault of a steel manu-
facturer; the bust of a dandified gentleman with hair
parted in the middle: the master of a dancing school.
The statue of a woman in an attitude of despair who
raises her arms towards the portrait in relief of her hus-
band.] A long way away a small group seems to be
gathered together on some very private business.* MARTINS
*is walking down the avenue towards them still carrying
his bag. Still further away stands a man in a mackintosh.
He stands there more like an observer than a participant
in the scene. He is* CALLOWAY. MARTINS *comes up to
him.*

MARTINS *quietly*: Could you tell me . . . is this . . .?

CALLOWAY *not at all moved*: A fellow called Lime.

As MARTINS *approaches the group, we can see a coffin
is on the point of being lowered into a grave and we hear
a passage of prayer the* PRIEST *is saying at the grave.*

PRIEST *mumbling rapidly*: Anima ejus, et animae omnium
fidelium defunctorum, per misericordiam Dei requiescant in
pace.

*Two men in heavy overcoats stand close to the grave.
One carries a wreath that he has obviously forgotten to
lay on the coffin, until his companion touches his elbow,
and he comes to with a start. A girl stands a little distance
away from them and she puts her hands over her face
as the coffin is lowered. We shall know her later as* ANNA
SCHMIDT.

MARTINS *stands watching the scene with tears gathering
in his eyes. (Still on page 18) The* PRIEST *puts a spoon of
earth on the coffin, and then the two men do the same.
·One of the men approaches the girl and offers her the
spoon. The girl shakes her head and turns away with tears
in her eyes. The man is left holding the spoon uncertainly.*
MARTINS *approaches him and takes the spoon from him
and adds his earth to the others. All the time* CALLOWAY
*watches the scene from a distance. The two men, whom
we know later on as* KURTZ *and* WINKEL, *stand side by*

side watching MARTINS, *whom they have never seen before; they are uneasy and puzzled. As he turns away from the grave, they say something to each other in low voices. The* PRIEST *goes up to them, speaks a few words and shakes their hands; he turns to* MARTINS, *but* MARTINS *is walking rapidly away. He stumbles on a loose stone as he walks.* CALLOWAY *follows him, catching him up.*

CALLOWAY *loudly :* I've got a car here. Like a lift to town?

MARTINS *stares at this man who offers him a lift as if they were leaving a party.*

MARTINS : [No] thanks.

*He starts to walk ahead, then changes his mind and returns to the taxi. As they get in, a jeep in the background, driven by a sergeant (*PAINE, *whom we meet later) who is watching. He starts up and follows.*

11. INT. TAXI : BACK PROJECTION (DAY) :

CALLOWAY *looks back towards the group by the grave, but* MARTINS *stares straight ahead.*

CALLOWAY : My name's Calloway.

MARTINS *does not at first answer; his thoughts are elsewhere.*

MARTINS : Martins.

CALLOWAY : You a friend of Lime? MARTINS *will not answer.* Been here long? [I haven't seen you around.]

[*No reaction from* MARTINS.][2] CALLOWAY *sees someone out of the window of the taxi and leans forward to get a better view.*

12. MAIN ROAD : LOCATION (DAY) :

The girl who was at the graveside is walking towards the city by the wall of the cemetery, with the trams running beside it. Behind are rows of monumental masons and flower shops, grave-stones waiting for the owners and wreaths for mourners.

13. TAXI : BACK PROJECTION (DAY) :

CALLOWAY *is now looking out of the back window at the receding figure. He turns to* MARTINS, *who is staring*

---

[2] In the film, MARTINS replies ' No.'

straight ahead, and speaks with a voice out of mood with the situation.

CALLOWAY : You've had a bit of a shock, haven't you? *No notice taken.* You need a drink.

For the first time, at the word ' drink' he gets a reaction.

MARTINS : Could you buy me one? I haven't got any Austrian money.

CALLOWAY : Of course.

As he leans forward to give the driver instructions, dissolve.

14. KARNTNERSTRASSE BAR (DAY):

A small bar consisting of two rooms. A self-absorbed courting couple sit in the first room. CALLOWAY *and* MARTINS *with his back to the entrance. A bottle of cognac is on the table and at intervals* CALLOWAY *fills* MARTINS's *glass, always giving him a little more than he does himself.* MARTINS *is already half-drunk. He twirls the bottom of his glass through the spilt drink on the table.*

MARTINS : I guess there's nobody knew Harry like he did . . . *Corrects himself* . . . like I did.

CALLOWAY's *lighter stays a moment half-way to his cigarette.*

CALLOWAY : How long ago?

MARTINS : First term at school. Never felt so damned lonely in my life — and then Harry showed up . . . [showed me the ropes.

He takes a swallow of brandy and spills some from his glass. Dipping his fingers in the spilled brandy he anoints himself on the top of the head and behind each ear.

MARTINS : He even taught me that.]

CALLOWAY : When did you see him last?

MARTINS : September '39. When the business started.[3]

CALLOWAY : See much of him before that?

MARTINS : Once in a while. [Once a month we might get pie-eyed — for the good of our health.]

[CALLOWAY : What were you going to do here?

MARTINS : You know this medical thing . . . this unit he ran?

---

[3] In the film, this line is given to CALLOWAY.

CALLOWAY: Not exactly — no . . .

MARTINS: Some sort of charity organisation which helped to get medical supplies. That was him, you know. Anyway he asked me to write some propaganda for him. I guess he knew I was broke. *His thoughts coming back to* LIME. It seems like yesterday — that school corridor and the cracked bell and all those British children kidding me about my accent.

CALLOWAY: And Lime?

MARTINS: He and I got up to a lot of things. *He laughs ruefully.* I was always the one who got caught.

CALLOWAY: That was convenient for Lime.

MARTINS *reaching the point of alcoholic irritation*: What are you getting at?

CALLOWAY: Well, wasn't it?

> *He is watching* MARTINS'S *reactions closely. He is dead sober, and we begin to notice the little barbed shafts he is sticking in* MARTINS'S *sides. He wants to make his bull angry.*

MARTINS: That was my fault. He was the . . . *circling the stem of the glass again.*] Best friend I ever had.

CALLOWAY: That sounds like a cheap novelette.

MARTINS: I *write* cheap novelettes.

CALLOWAY: I've never heard of you. What's your name again?

MARTINS: Rollo Martins.[4]

CALLOWAY: No. Sorry.

MARTINS [*used to not being known*: You know, I don't write masterpieces, I don't like masterpieces.] *As English as possible.* Ever heard of 'The Lone Rider of Santa Fe'?

CALLOWAY: No.

MARTINS *very American*: 'Death at Double X Ranch'?

CALLOWAY: No.

MARTINS: [Nobody reads Westerns nowadays. Harry liked them though.][5] It's a damned shame.

CALLOWAY: What?

MARTINS: Him dying like that.

---

[4] In the film, he is called Holly instead of Rollo.

[5] In the film, MARTINS adds: 'Must have known I was broke — even sent me an aeroplane ticket.'

Calloway : The best thing that ever happened to him.
[Martins *hazy with drink* : You mean — being killed quick.
Calloway : He was lucky in that way too. *He is now speaking in a deliberately insulting way.*]

>   Martins *at last sees that there is a hidden meaning in* Calloway's *words. He becomes quieter and more dangerous. His right hand lets go of the brandy glass and lies on the table ready for action.*

Martins : What are you trying to say?

>   Calloway *knows what is coming. He moves his chair very slowly back, calculating* Martins's *reach. Still on page 17)*

Calloway : You see, he'd have served a long spell — if it hadn't been for the accident.

Martins : What for?

Calloway : He was about the worst racketeer who ever made a dirty living in this city. Have another drink.

Martins : You some sort of a policeman?

Calloway *sitting back* : Mmm.[6]

Martins : I don't like policemen.

>   Martins *edges his chair round to block* Calloway's *way out;* Calloway *catches the waiter's eye. The waiter obviously knows what is expected of him and goes out.*

Martins *gently with a surface smile* : I have to call them sheriffs.

Calloway : Ever seen one?

Martins : You're the first. I guess there was some petty racket going on with gasoline and you couldn't pin it on anyone, so you picked a dead man. Just like a cop. You're a real cop, I suppose?

Calloway : Yes, but it wasn't petrol.

Martins : Tyres?[7] . . . Saccharine? . . . Why don't you catch a few murderers for a change?

Calloway : Well, you could say that murder was part of his racket.

>   Martins *pushes the table over with one hand and makes*

---

[6] In the film, Calloway adds: ' Have another drink.'

[7] In the film, Martins begins: ' So it wasn't petrol? So it was (tyres).

a dive at CALLOWAY *with the other: the drink confuses his calculations. Before he can try, his arms are caught behind him. Neither we nor* MARTINS *have seen the entrance of Sergeant* PAINE, *who has been summoned by the waiter and who now pinions* MARTINS.

CALLOWAY : [Don't treat him roughly.][8] He's only a scribbler with too much drink in him. *With contempt.* Take Mr. Rollo Martins home.

PAINE *impressed* : Rollo Martins, sir? MARTINS *struggles.* [Be quiet, can't you, sir.] *To* CALLOWAY. The writer? ' The Lone Rider of Santa Fe '?

CALLOWAY *nods and moves away to collect his mackintosh.*

MARTINS : Listen, Callaghan, or whatever your name is . . .

CALLOWAY : Calloway. I'm English, not Irish.

MARTINS : There's one dead man you aren't going to pin your unsolved crimes on.

CALLOWAY : Going to find me the real criminal? It sounds like one of your stories.

MARTINS : You can let me go, Callaghan. If I gave you a black eye, you'd only go to bed for a few days. When I've finished with you — you'll leave Vienna, you'll look so silly.

CALLOWAY *takes out a couple of pounds' worth of Bafs and sticks them in* MARTINS' *breast pocket.*

CALLOWAY : This is Army money. Should see you through tonight at Sacher's Hotel if you don't spend too much in the bar. We'll keep a seat for you on tomorrow's plane.

[MARTINS : You can't throw me out. My papers are in order.

CALLOWAY : This is like other cities : you need money here. Let him go.

PAINE *lets go of his arms and dusts* MARTINS *down.*

MARTINS : I'd thank you for the drinks — but I guess they were on expenses.

CALLOWAY : Yes.]

MARTINS [*steps to one side as though to make way for the waiter and*] *slashes out at* CALLOWAY. [CALLOWAY *just avoids him, but stumbles against the table.*] *Before* MARTINS *can try again,* PAINE, *who has been greatly*

---

[8] In the film, CALLOWAY begins: That's all right, Paine.'

impressed by meeting MARTINS, *has to land him on the mouth. He* [*goes bang over in the alleyway between the tables and*] *comes up bleeding from a cut lip.*

[CALLOWAY : You promised not to fight.]

PAINE *lifts him up and dusts him down again.*

PAINE : Please be careful, sir.[9] Written anything lately?

MARTINS *wipes some of the blood away with his sleeve.*

CALLOWAY *has had a long day and is tired of* MARTINS.

CALLOWAY : Take him to Sacher's. Don't hit him again if he behaves. You go carefully there —it's a Military Hotel.

CALLOWAY *turns away from both of them and leaves the bar.*

PAINE *still dusting* MARTINS *down* : I'm so glad to have met you, sir. [I know all your books.] *He leads* MARTINS *towards the door — he holds his arm — he carries his bag and smiles to him.* I like a good Western.[10] *Dissolve.*

15. SACHER'S HOTEL LOUNGE (DAY) :

Sacher's Hotel, which may roughly be compared to Brown's Hotel in London, has been taken over by the British Army, but this has not altered its atmosphere of red plush and Edwardian pictures, nor the old world courtesy of the porter who treats every subaltern like a grand duke. [*Two men with a distinctly ex-officer look are having tea. Their lounge suits have rather a mothball air, and their faces are anxious. Their names are* CARTER *and* TOMBS. TOMBS *is the more pessimistic and saturnine.* CARTER *gives an appearance of ill-directed energy. A young* OFFICER *passes by them.*

OFFICER : Hello, you chaps, how's the culture going?

TOMBS : It's an uphill climb, old man.

OFFICER : Heard you were going to be back in uniform next week.

He picks up a biscuit off their tea tray.

CARTER : That joke's in the worst possible taste.

OFFICER: Hear the Brigadier didn't like last week's striptease.

---

[9] In the film, PAINE adds : ' Up we come.'

[10] In the film, PAINE says : ' We read quite a few of your books. I like a good Western. That's what I like about them, sir, pick them up and put them down any time.'

TOMBS : It wasn't striptease. It was Hindu dancing.

The OFFICER *moves on, munching their biscuit.*

TOMBS : Sometimes, old man, one gets discouraged.

CARTER : Tombs, do you think there's anything in what he said?

TOMBS : Frankly, yes.

CARTER : After all we've done for re-education.

TOMBS : It would seem strange to be in uniform again.

He shivers slightly and his cup shakes.

CARTER : Don't . . . If only we could put on one really good show.

TOMBS : I saw nothing wrong with last week's. Perhaps they should have had a larger loin cloth.

A SENIOR OFFICER *enters with a* WOMAN.

TOMBS *in a whisper*: Don't look round. Slip quietly out, old man. It's the Brigadier.

They leave with the utmost caution.][11]

16. SACHER'S RECEPTION HALL (DAY):

PAINE *leads* MARTINS *to the hall porter's desk. He is carrying* MARTINS'S *bag for him, and* MARTINS *has a handkerchief pressed to his mouth.* [CARTER *and* TOMBS *approach from the lounge.*]

PAINE *to the* PORTER : Colonel Calloway says this gentleman is to have a bed for the night.

[PORTER : Your passport, please.]

As MARTINS *is producing it,* PAINE *moves over to* CARTER *and* TOMBS *who are staring at this strange-looking tourist.*

PAINE : Rollo Martins, sir, the writer. Thought you'd be interested.

[TOMBS *turning away* : Never heard of him.]

CARTER : Did you say *writer*, Paine?

TOMBS *turns back.*

PAINE : Of books, sir. Yes, Westerns, sir.[12] [*Very seriously.* I enjoyed the striptease last week, sir.]

[*As* PAINE *moves back to the desk,* CARTER *and* TOMBS

---

[11] In the film, CARTER and TOMBS are amalgamated into one character named CRABBIT.

[12] In the film, PAINE adds: 'He's very good, sir. We read quite a few of his books.'

both stare at MARTINS.

PAINE *to* MARTINS : Good night, sir, I hope you'll be comfortable.

MARTINS *nods good night, as the porter gives* MARTINS *the usual papers to sign.*

CARTER *doubtfully* : A writer, Tombs.

TOMBS : Not very high class, old man.

CARTER : Well, they're books, aren't they? We've got to take a chance.

TOMBS : I've got a foreboding.

CARTER : You chose the Hindu dancing, Tombs. Leave this to me.

He approaches MARTINS *who is receiving his key at the desk.* TOMBS *lags a little way behind.*]

CARTER : Mr. Martins, isn't it?

MARTINS : Yes.

[CARTER : My name's Carter — Captain Carter, and this is Tombs — Captain Tombs.

MARTINS : Yes?

CARTER : We run the C.R.S. of G.H.Q., you know.

MARTINS : You do?

CARTER : Cultural Re-education Section. Directly I heard you were here, I thought — there's the man for us. We are having a little discussion at our Institute the day after to-morrow on the — well, you know, the usual literary subjects. Sort of lecture, you know — we thought you might like to speak.

MARTINS : They wouldn't know me.

CARTER : Nonsense, your books are very popular here —aren't they, Tombs?

TOMBS : Staying here long, Mr. Martins?][13]

---

[13] In the film, the following sequence is substituted :
CRABBIT : The name's Crabbit. I represent the C.R.S. of G.H.Q., you know.
MARTINS : You do?
CRABBIT : Cultural Re-education Section. Propaganda — very important in a place like this. We do a little show each week — last week we had 'Hamlet'. Week before we had — um . . . something . . .
PAINE : The striptease, sir.

MARTINS *showing Bafs* : How long can you stay on a couple of pounds of this funny money?

CARTER : We'd like you to be our guest, sir. Glad to have you here.

MARTINS : Did you say . . . guest?

CARTER : As long as you care to stay.

[TOMBS *in an undertone* : Careful.

CARTER : But, of course, do say yes — it is really great fun — isn't it, Tombs?

TOMBS : Great.

MARTINS *speaking into his handkerchief* : Okay.][14]

TOMBS : Got toothache, sir? I know a very good dentist.

MARTINS : I don't need a dentist. Somebody hit me, that's all.

CARTER : Trying to rob you?

MARTINS : Just a soldier.

> MARTINS *removes the handkerchief and gives them a view.*

[CARTER : American?

MARTINS : British. I punched his colonel in the eye.

TOMBS *smiling* : Really, a colonel?

MARTINS : I came here to stay with a friend of mine.][15] And he died last Thursday — then . . .

CRABBIT: Oh yes, the Hindu Dancers, thank you, sergeant. This is the first opportunity we've had of making an American author welcome.

MARTINS: Welcome?

CRABBIT: I'll tell you what, on Wednesday night at our Institute, we're having a little lecture on the — er — contemporary novel. Perhaps you'd like to speak?

MARTINS: They wouldn't know me.

CRABBIT: Oh nonsense, your novels are very popular here, aren't they, sergeant?

PAINE: Very popular.

CRABBIT: Very popular. Are you staying long?

[14] In the film, PAINE adds: 'But he's due to leave tomorrow, sir.'

[15] In the film, the sequence is adapted:
MARTINS: I was trying to punch his major in the eye.
CRABBIT *smiling*: Really, a major?
MARTINS: Heard of Harry Lime? I came here to stay with him.

CARTER : Goodness, that's awkward.

MARTINS : Is that what you say to people after a death? Goodness, that's awkward!

PORTER *holding up telephone*: Mr. Martins, excuse me, Baron von Kurtz.

MARTINS : It's a mistake.

> *But he takes the telephone.* CARTER *and* PAINE *move a little away and converse together in undertones.*

MARTINS : Yes.

VOICE : I was a friend of Harry Lime.

MARTINS *his attitude changing*: I would much like to meet you, Baron. Come around.

VOICE : Austrians aren't allowed in Sacher's. May we meet at the Mozart Café? Just around the corner.

MARTINS : How will I know you?

VOICE : I'll carry a copy of one of your books. *He sniggers.* Harry gave it to me.

MARTINS : Be there in a moment.

> *He hangs up and goes over to* CARTER.

MARTINS : If I do this, I can be your guest for a week? Can I?

CARTER : Certainly. You're just the man we need.

MARTINS : Fine. *He starts for the door, excited, then turns.* Ever read a book of mine called 'The Lone Rider of Santa Fe'?

CARTER : No . . . *Trying to remember* . . . Not that one. [. . . *Turns to* TOMBS . . . Did you? TOMBS *cannot help.*

TOMBS : I don't think so.]

MARTINS : This lone rider has his best friend shot unlawfully by a sheriff. The story is how this lone rider hunted that sheriff down.

TOMBS : Sounds exciting.

MARTINS : It is. I'm gunning just the same way for your Colonel Callaghan.[16]

---

[16] In the film, all MARTINS's preceding four speeches are adapted:
MARTINS says: (1) 'If I do this (lecture business) . . .'
(2) 'Fine. (It's a deal.)'
(3) 'Story about a rider who hunted down a sheriff who was victimizing his best friend.'
(4) 'Colonel Callaghan' is called 'Major Calloway.'

As MARTINS *turns to the door,* PAINE *speaks uneasily to* CARTER.

PAINE : Sounds anti-British, [old boy.

CARTER : So were your Hindu dancers.]

17. MOZART CAFE. PART LOCATION (DAY):

MARTINS *enters the café and examines the occupants. Several are reading newspapers — they do not interest him. He passes over a group playing cards, but there remain two or three, reading books, and the audience is given time to decide for themselves which of these is* KURTZ: *the young man with the arrogant Hitler these is* KURTZ : *the young man with the arrogant Hitler Jugend look about him?* MARTINS *passes by to catch his eye — looks as if ready to smile — he gets no reaction. He turns away and at that moment* KURTZ *enters the café.* MARTINS *recognizes him at once because he holds well to the fore the gaudy paper-covered Western with a picture of a cowboy leaping from a horse onto the horns of a galloping steer. He wears a toupée, flat and yellow with the hair out straight at the back and not fitting close. He carries a stick with an ivory top.* MARTINS *meets him.*[17]

MARTINS : Baron Kurtz?

KURTZ : Martins? Delighted to meet you.

His English accent is really too good. A man ought not to speak a foreign language so well.

KURTZ : Let us sit here. [This is my usual seat. I come here, you know, out of the cold . . .]

His clothes are shabby, but not too shabby. His overcoat looks quite adequate compared with the poor clothes of the other men. When they are seated, he calls a waiter and orders coffee. That done, he leans back with a sigh.

KURTZ : It's wonderful how you keep the tension.

MARTINS : Tension?

KURTZ : Suspense. At the end of every chapter, you are left guessing . . . what he'll be up to next.

[MARTINS : You really liked it?

KURTZ : The best I've read of yours.

---

[17] In the film, these descriptions of atmosphere are caught in essence, if not to the letter.

The waiter brings the coffee, and KURTZ *takes out of his waistcoat pocket an elegant little 18th century snuff box.*

KURTZ : A saccharine tablet?

MARTINS : Thank you. There's only one left!

KURTZ : Oh, dear. I knew I was short, but I don't take sweetening myself. I carry them for my friends.

He takes a small leather-bound notebook out of his pocket and makes a note.

KURTZ : My memory is so bad.]

MARTINS : So you were a friend of Harry's?

KURTZ : I think his best. *A small pause in which his brain must have registered the error.* Except you, of course.

MARTINS : The police have a crazy notion that he was mixed up in some racket. (*Still on page 18*)

KURTZ : Everyone in Vienna is — we all sell cigarettes and that kind of thing. Why, I have done things that would have seemed unthinkable before the war. Once when I was hard up, I sold some tyres on the black market. I wonder what my father would have said.

MARTINS : The police meant something worse.

[KURTZ: Sometimes they get things mixed. Who was that man at the cemetery who spoke to you?

MARTINS : He's the one — the policeman who made Harry out to be every kind of crook.]

KURTZ : They get rather absurd ideas sometimes.

[MARTINS : They can't monkey around with Harry even if he's dead.]

KURTZ : He's somewhere now he won't mind about that.

MARTINS : Well, anyway, I'm not going to leave it at this — will you help me?

KURTZ *has a cup of coffee halfway to his lips; he takes a slow sip.*

KURTZ : [One begins to forget what real Vienna coffee tasted like.]¹⁸ You know I am an Austrian — I have to be careful with the police; no, I can't help you — except with advice, of course, advice.

[MARTINS : I'm bad at taking that.

---

¹⁸ In the film, KURTZ begins : ' I wish I could.'

Pause. MARTINS *glances at* KURTZ, *feeling that* HARRY'S *friend should be more helpful.*]

MARTINS : Well, anyway, show me how it happened.
Dissolve.

18. OUTSIDE LIME'S FLAT. LOCATION (DAY):
KURTZ *is standing at the door of* LIME'S *flat, and is holding* MARTINS'S *arm.*

KURTZ: You see, you might be Harry. We came out like this and were walking this way . . .
He points to a doorway on the other side of the road; the camera follows imaginary figures while the voice continues.

KURTZ: An [American] friend of his, Tyler,[19] called to him from over there. Harry went across, and from up there . . . *Points down the road* . . . came the truck. It was Harry's fault, really, not the driver's. *Looking down on the ground.* It was just about here.
[*The noise of an approaching truck sounds like an illustration to* KURTZ'S *story, but as he utters the last words, he pulls* MARTINS *on one side and a real truck drives quickly by.*]

KURTZ : These military cars aren't safe.

MARTINS : It was here?
He kicks with his foot at a broken stone on the kerb. From out of the doorway to HARRY'S *flat comes the* PORTER *sweeping the steps. They nod to each other.* KURTZ *sees this.*

KURTZ: Tyler and I carried him across to the doorway over there. *He leads* MARTINS *to the other side of the road. The* PORTER *continues sweeping with his eyes on the two of them.*

19. [DOORWAY. PART LOCATION (DAY):
It leads to some cheap apartments. There are a couple of dustbins in the porch.][20]

KURTZ : And this is where he died. [MARTINS *takes in the dreary doorway and the dustbins.*] Even at the end his thoughts were of you.

---

19 In the film, the American TYLER is the Rumanian POPESCU.
20 This location is changed to near a statue of the Emperor Franz Josef in the middle of the square.

MARTINS *greatly moved*: What did he say?

KURTZ: I can't remember the exact words. Rollo — I may call you Rollo, mayn't I? — he always called you that to us — he was anxious I should look after you when you arrived — to see that you got safely home. Tickets, you know, and all that.

MARTINS *indicating* PORTER: He told me he died instantaneously.

KURTZ: No. But he died before the ambulance could reach us.

[MARTINS: There was an inquest?

KURTZ: Of course. The driver was exonerated. It really was Harry's fault.]

MARTINS: So you were here, and this man Tyler. I'd like to talk to him.

KURTZ: He's left Vienna.

> MARTINS *walks across to the* PORTER.

MARTINS: You remember me?

PORTER: Yes.

MARTINS: I wanted to ask you some questions about Harry Lime.

> *The* PORTER'S WIFE *has come out and gives an angry look at* MARTINS *and* KURTZ.[21]

PORTER'S WIFE *in German*: Don't stand there gossiping.

> *She hustles him in.* MARTINS *returns thoughtfully to* KURTZ.

MARTINS: Who was at the funeral besides you?

KURTZ: Only his doctor, Dr. Winkel.

MARTINS: The girl?

KURTZ: Oh, you know what Harry was. Some girl from the Josefstadt Theatre. *He sees an intention in* MARTINS'S *face and adds quickly.* You oughtn't to speak to her. It would only cause her pain.

MARTINS: We don't have to think about her. We've got to

---

[21] In the film, the following sequence is added:
MARTINS: Who used to visit Mr. Lime?
> *The* PORTER *speaks to* KURTZ *in German.*
MARTINS: What's he say?
KURTZ: He says he doesn't know everybody.

think about Harry.

KURTZ: What's the good of another post mortem? Suppose you dig up something — well, discreditable to Harry?

MARTINS *shakes his head. It is not an idea he will entertain.*

MARTINS: Could I have your address?

KURTZ: I live in the Russian Sector. [One has to work the best way one can, you know. Poor mother — I keep it from her.][22]

MARTINS: What was the girl's name?

KURTZ: I don't know. I don't think I ever heard it.

MARTINS: But the theatre where she works?

KURTZ: The Josefstadt. I still think it won't do Harry any good. You'd do better to think of yourself.

MARTINS: I'll be all right.

They turn to go.

KURTZ: I'm glad to have met you, Rollo.

KURTZ *holds up the book showing the cowboy on the cover.*

KURTZ: A master of suspense. Such a good cover, I think.

[KURTZ *leads the way from the porch. As he steps onto the pavement an Austrian police officer approaches, and* KURTZ *makes way for him with sudden subservience as they walk down the street.*] *Dissolve.*

20. SACHER'S HOTEL: RECEPTION DESK (DAY):
MARTINS *comes in and finds Sergeant* PAINE *waiting.* PAINE *advances to meet him and holds out an envelope.*

PAINE: Colonel Calloway sent this, with his compliments. It's the ticket for the plane tomorrow. He said I was to drive you out to the airfield or take you to the bus, whichever you prefer.

MARTINS: Tell Colonel Calloway I won't need it.[23] *He hands the ticket back to the sergeant and turns to the porter.* Please get me a ticket for the Josefstadt theatre tonight.

He walks slowly up the staircase one step at a time —

---

22 In the film, KURTZ adds: 'But you'll find me at the Casanova Club every night.'

23 In the film, MARTINS adds: 'Didn't you hear Mister Crabbit offer me the hospitality of the H.Q.B.M.C.?'

feeling he has started to put CALLOWAY *in his place.*
Dissolve.

21. JOSEFSTADT THEATRE (NIGHT):
MARTINS *is seated in the stalls. A play is in progress. He cannot understand a word of it, and gazes bewilderedly at his neighbours when they rock with laughter at a situation which visually seems serious enough. On the stage an elderly man and a woman are enough. On the stage an elderly man and a woman are storming at a girl — the girl from the cemetery [all the easier to recognise because she wears the same mackintosh as she did there]*[24] *— who protests something, he does not know what. At every sentence, the audience howls with laughter. He looks at his programme and we see the name of* ANNA SCHMIDT. *As he looks up at the stage again, the curtain falls. The audience remain in their seats, but* MARTINS *scrambles out and through the small door at one side of the stage.*

22. BACKSTAGE. LOCATION (NIGHT):
A quick change of scene is taking place on the stage. MARTINS *watches from the wings the scene-shifters at work.* ANNA SCHMIDT *comes up hurriedly and stands near him, doing up her dress: the clasps will not fasten — she does not notice him.*
[MARTINS : Fraulein Schmidt?
ANNA : Yes? *She glances up at him and back to her dress.*]
MARTINS : I was a friend of Harry Lime.
ANNA *stops and stares at him. The curtain is rising and her entrance has to be on the rise of the curtain.*
ANNA *quickly*: Afterwards. Afterwards.
She goes onto the stage and, playing her first lines towards him, watches with an expression, puzzled and distressed, the stranger who has broken into her grief. For the first time we really take her in: an honest face: a wide forehead, a large mouth which does not try to charm, the kind of face which you can recognise at once as a friend's. The opening lines of this scene demand that she should approach the wings. Dissolve.

---
[24] In the film, the actors all wear eighteenth century costume.

23. ANNA'S DRESSING ROOM (NIGHT):
ANNA *opens the door to* MARTINS. [*Unlike most actresses'
rooms, this one is almost bare: no wardrobe packed with
clothes, no clutter of cosmetics and greasepaint: a
sweater on the door one recognises from the first act.*]
*On the only easy chair, a tin of half-used paints and
grease. A kettle hums softly on a gas ring.*[25]
MARTINS : My name's Rollo Martins. Perhaps Harry told
you about me.
ANNA : No. He never told me about his friends.
[MARTINS : I think I was his oldest.]
ANNA : Would you like a cup of tea? Someone threw me a
packet last week — sometimes the British do, instead of
flowers, you know, on the first night.
*She opens a cupboard under the dressing table to get
the tea and shows a bottle of Canadian Club.*
ANNA : That was a bouquet too, from an American. *Reluct-
antly.* Would you rather have a whisky?
MARTINS : Tea's okay.
ANNA : Good. *She closes the cupboard.* I wanted to sell it.
*He watches her while she makes the tea. All wrong: the
water not on the boil, the teapot unheated, too few leaves.
She pours it out immediately.*
[ANNA : I never understand why the English like tea.
MARTINS : Oh, I like it.] You'd known him some time?
Her mouth stiffens to meet the dreaded conversation.
ANNA : Yes.
MARTINS : I knew him twenty years. *Gently.* I want to talk
to you about him . . .
ANNA *stares back at him.*
ANNA : There's nothing really to talk about, is there? Nothing.
*He drinks his cup quickly like a medicine and watches
her gingerly and delicately sip at hers.*

---

[25] In the film, the following sequence is added:
MARTINS *at the door*: Miss Schmidt?
ANNA: Come in.
MARTINS: I enjoyed the play very much. You were awfully good .
ANNA: You understand German?
MARTINS: No — no — I . . . excuse me, I could follow it fine.

MARTINS : I saw you at the funeral.

ANNA : I'm sorry . . . I didn't notice much.

MARTINS : You loved him, didn't you?

ANNA : I don't know. You can't know a thing like that — afterwards. I don't know anything any more except . . . *She hesitates;* MARTINS *looks at her.* I want to be dead too. *There is silence for a while.* Another cup of tea?

MARTINS *too promptly*: No, no thank you . . . Cigarette? *He offers a Lucky Strike packet.*

ANNA : Thank you . . . I like Americans.

> *He lights it, but during the following scene she lets it go out.*

MARTINS : I've been talking to a friend of Harry's. Baron Kurtz. Do you know him?

ANNA : No.

MARTINS : He wears a *toupée*. I can't understand what Harry saw in him.

ANNA : Oh, yes. *She does not like him.* That was the man who brought me some money when Harry died. He said Harry had been anxious — at the last moment.

MARTINS : He must have been very clear in his head at the end : he remembered about me too. It seems to show there wasn't really any pain.

ANNA : Doctor Winkel told me that . . .

MARTINS : Who's he?

ANNA : A doctor Harry used to go to. He was passing just after it happened.

MARTINS : Harry's own doctor?

ANNA : Yes.

MARTINS : Did you go to the inquest?

ANNA : Yes. They said it wasn't the driver's fault. Harry had often said what a careful driver he was.

MARTINS *astonished* : He was Harry's driver?

ANNA : Yes.

MARTINS : I don't get this. Kurtz and [the American] — his own driver knocking him down — his own doctor — not a single stranger.

> *He is brooding on this new fact.*

ANNA : I've wondered about it a hundred times — if it really was an accident. MARTINS *is astonished.* What difference does it make? He's dead.

VOICE *from outside* : Fraulein Schmidt.

ANNA : They don't like us to use the light. It uses up their electricity.

MARTINS *up to this point had never thought of murder.*
MARTINS : The porter saw it happen. It couldn't have been . . .[26]

Dissolve.

24. HARRY'S FLAT. SITTING ROOM (NIGHT):
The PORTER *throws open the window.* MARTINS *stands behind him.* ANNA *is a little distance away, examining the room as though it was a home to which she had returned after many years.*

PORTER : It happened right down there.
He leans out and we look down with him to the pavement five storeys below. ANNA *turns abruptly away and walks through an open door into the bedroom.*

MARTINS : And you saw it?

PORTER : Well, not saw. I heard it though. I heard the brakes put on and the sound of the skid and I got to the window and saw them carry the body to the other side of the [road][27] . . .
He points . . . over there.
While the PORTER *is talking,* MARTINS *turns and watches* ANNA *in the next room.*

25. BEDROOM (NIGHT):
She stands beside the bed with her head down, and every now and then she raises it and takes a quick look here and there.

26. SITTING ROOM (NIGHT):
MARTINS *says in a low voice so as not to carry to the next room . . .*

MARTINS : Could he have been conscious?

PORTER : Oh no, he was quite dead.

MARTINS : I've been told he *didn't* die at once.

---

[26] In the film, MARTINS adds: 'You know that porter?' And ANNA replies: 'Yes.'

[27] In the film, the PORTER adds: 'Emperor Josef statue . . .'

PORTER: He couldn't have been alive, not with his head in the state it was.[28]

27. BEDROOM (NIGHT):

ANNA *moves from the bed. Twice she puts out her hand and touches the wall. She comes to the dressing table. In the mirror is stuck a snapshot. It is of herself, laughing into the camera. Above it she sees her face in the mirror with tousled hair and hopeless eyes. Automatically she puts her hand down to the right hand drawer. She does not have to look. She opens the drawer and pulls out a comb. Still only half-conscious of what she is doing, she raises it to her head and is just going to use the comb when her eye falls on something in the drawer belonging to* HARRY. *She drops the comb, slams the drawer to, and puts her hand over her face.*

28. SITTING ROOM (NIGHT):

MARTINS: Why didn't you say all this at the Inquest?

PORTER: It's better not to be mixed up in things like that.

MARTINS: [It was your duty.][29]

PORTER: I was not the only one who did not give evidence.

MARTINS: What do you mean?

PORTER: Three men helped to carry your friend to the [house.][30]

MARTINS: No — only Kurtz and the American.

PORTER: There was a third man. He didn't give evidence.

MARTINS: *Three* men carried the body?

PORTER: Yes. The third one held his head.

MARTINS: You don't mean the doctor?

PORTER: Oh no, he didn't arrive till after they got him to the doorway.

MARTINS: Can't you describe this — third man?

---

[28] In the film, the following sequence is added:
PORTER *trying to explain*: Wait a moment, Fraulein Schmidt. *He asks her a question in German.*
ANNA: He was quite dead.
PORTER: He was quite dead.
MARTINS: But this sounds crazy. If he was killed at once, how could he have talked about me and this lady after he was dead?
[29] In the film, MARTINS says: ' Things like what? '
[30] In the film, it is ' statue.'

PORTER : No. He didn't look up. He was just — ordinary. He might have been anybody.

MARTINS looks down at the pavement. At the PORTER'S last sentence, MARTINS looks down at two or three people passing foreshortened on the pavement.

MARTINS *almost to himself* : Just anybody. But I think he murdered Harry.

A telephone starts to ring in the bedroom.

29. BEDROOM (NIGHT) :

ANNA picks up the receiver.

ANNA : Hallo, wer ist da? (Hello, who is there?)

There is no reply, but whoever it is remains on the line.

ANNA: Warum antworten Sie nicht? (Why don't you answer?)

She puts the receiver down and turns to MARTINS.

ANNA: Nobody. (Still on page 51)

MARTINS turns back into the other room.[31]

30. SITTING ROOM (NIGHT) :

The PORTER does not want to continue the discussion.

MARTINS : You've got to tell the police your story.

Through the open door of the room from the landing outside trickles a child's ball — nobody sees it.

PORTER : Nonsense. It is all nonsense. It was an accident. I saw it happen.

A child (little HANSL) comes to the door and looks in — the ball is too far across the floor for him to reach it unobserved — and he skulks there, watching the scene, waiting his opportunity.

MARTINS : Be accurate. You saw a dead man and three men carrying him.

The PORTER is working himself up from self-protection into rage.

PORTER : You have no business forcing your way in here and talking nonsense. I ought to have listened to my wife. She said you were up to no good. Gossip.

MARTINS : Don't you see your evidence is important?

PORTER : I have no evidence. I saw nothing. I'm not concerned. You must go at once please. Fraulein Anna.

---

[31] In the film, MARTINS begins: ' But I was told there were only two men there.'

43

ANNA SCHMIDT *comes in from the bedroom.*

ANNA : What is it?

PORTER : ~~I have always liked you, Fraulein Anna, whatever~~
my wife may say, but you must not bring this gentleman
again.

> *The* PORTER *shepherds them towards the door. The child
> backs out of sight onto the landing — as the* PORTER
> *reaches the ball and kicks it angrily through the door — it
> bounces into the corridor and off down the stairs. The
> child follows it. Dissolve.*

31. ANNA'S STREET. LOCATION (NIGHT) :
> ANNA *and* MARTINS *walk up to the door of an ancient
> bombed house where* ANNA *has a room — she looks in
> her bag for the key.*[32]

32. DOORWAY. PART LOCATION (NIGHT).
> *The door of the house has been broken away and a make-
> shift door has been made out of planks nailed roughly
> together. Between the planks can be seen an* OLD
> WOMAN *hurrying towards the door. She starts to talk to*
> ANNA *excitedly in German. (Still on page 39) Through
> the cracks in the door,* ANNA *steps back on the pavement
> and looks up to a lighted window.*

MARTINS : What is it?

ANNA : The Police.[33]

33. HALLWAY AND STAIRCASE (NIGHT) :
> *A once grand house, badly bombed, and with half the
> walls out — a large staircase leads upstairs. The* OLD
> WOMAN *follows behind* ANNA *and* MARTINS, *to whom
> she behaves like a hostess; muttering all the time and not
> able to keep up with them; and stops on the first landing,
> watching up . . .*

34. STAIRCASE AND LANDING (NIGHT) :
> ANNA'S *bedroom had once been a reception room; it is
> large with a high ceiling, but is now a cheaply-furnished*

---

[32] In the film, the following sequence is added :
ANNA : You shouldn't get mixed up in this.
MARTINS : Well, if I do find out something, can I look you up again?
ANNA : Why don't you leave this town — go home?

[33] In the film, ANNA adds : ' They are searching my room.'

room with the bare necessities. ANNA *and* MARTINS *can see nobody through the half-opened door, but the drawers of a chest are open, and her things are piled in neat heaps on top. Photographs have been removed from frames, etc. Reaction of bewilderment and fear on* ANNA'S *face.* MARTINS *swings the door open with his foot.*

35. ANNA'S BEDROOM (NIGHT):
The opening of the door has taken no one by surprise. CALLOWAY *stands inside while* PAINE *and two Austrian* POLICEMEN, *paying no attention whatever to the arrival of* ANNA *and* MARTINS, *continue their search.*

MARTINS : What the devil? . . .

CALLOWAY : Getting around, Martins?

MARTINS : Pinning things on girls now?

CALLOWAY *ignoring him* : I want to see your papers, Miss Schmidt.

MARTINS : Don't give him a thing.

ANNA *opens her bag, hands over her papers.*

CALLOWAY : Thank you.

He begins to turn them over.

[MARTINS : I'm going to your superiors . . . you'll find out . . .]

CALLOWAY : You were born in Graz, of Austrian parents? . . .

ANNA *in a low voice* : Yes.

CALLOWAY *lifts the document to the light and examines it at the level of his eyes.*

CALLOWAY : [Take a look,] Paine. PAINE *repeats the action.* See what I mean?

PAINE : Yes, sir.[34]

CALLOWAY : I'll have to keep these for a while, Miss Schmidt.

She is too scared to protest. MARTINS *does it for her.*

MARTINS : You can't go that far, Callaghan. She can't live in this city without papers.

CALLOWAY : Write her out a receipt, Paine. That will serve. Give her a receipt for the other things too.

---

[34] In the film, PAINE adds : ' It's very good, sir, isn't it? ' And CALLOWAY asks ANNA : ' How much did you pay for this? '

45

PAINE : This way, miss.

He leads the way through into the sitting-room.[35]

36. ANNA'S SITTING ROOM (NIGHT):

PAINE *seats himself at a table where a number of objects are already stacked, including a bundle of letters.*

ANNA : You aren't taking those?

PAINE *writing on a leaf of his notebook* : They'll be returned, miss.

ANNA : They are private letters.

PAINE : Don't worry, miss. We are used to it. Like doctors.

ANNA *leaves him and goes to the doorway.*

37. ANNA'S BEDROOM (NIGHT):

MARTINS *is in the middle of a tirade.* ANNA *listens.*

MARTINS : And there was a third man there. I suppose that doesn't sound peculiar to you.

CALLOWAY : I'm not interested in whether a racketeer like Lime was killed by his friends or in an accident. The only important thing is that he's dead.

As he speaks the last words, he turns and sees ANNA *in the doorway.*

CALLOWAY : I'm sorry.

MARTINS : [What an inhuman so-and-so you are, Callaghan.][36]

CALLOWAY *with good humour* : Calloway.

ANNA : Must you take those letters?

CALLOWAY : Yes, I'm afraid so.

ANNA : They are Harry's.

CALLOWAY : That's the reason.

ANNA : You won't learn anything from them. They are only — love letters. There are not many of them ...

CALLOWAY : They'll be returned, Miss Schmidt, after they've been examined.

ANNA : There's nothing in them. Harry never did anything. *She hesitates.* Only a small thing, once, out of kindness.

CALLOWAY : What was that?

ANNA *turning to the other room* : You've got it in your hand.

---

35 In the film, MARTINS asks: 'I suppose it doesn't interest you to hear Harry Lime was murdered?'

36 In the film, MARTINS says: 'Tactful too, aren't we, Callaghan?'

CALLOWAY *lifts his hand with* ANNA'S *papers in them.*
PAINE *comes through from the other room and hands*
ANNA *the receipt for her letters, etc.*

[PAINE : Shall we clean up for you, miss?
He makes to put one of the photographs back in its
frame.

ANNA *quickly, sharply* : No. Don't touch it again.]

CALLOWAY *to Austrian* POLICEMAN *in German* : Finished?

POLICEMAN *in German* : Nearly.

CALLOWAY : You'll have to come with us, Miss Schmidt.
Martins, go home like a sensible chap. You don't know what
you are mixing in. Get the next plane.

MARTINS : You can't order me around, Callaghan. I'm going
to get to the bottom of this.

CALLOWAY : Death's at the bottom of everything, Martins.
Leave death to the professionals.[37]

CALLOWAY *crosses to* PAINE, *where some of* ANNA'S
belongings are being put back. ANNA *goes to the chest*
and begins to put one of the photographs back in its
frame. MARTINS *watches it, and her. The photograph*
of a man grinning with great gaiety and vitality at the
camera.

MARTINS : That's him all right. He would have known how
to handle that . . . *Whispers* . . . Why did they take your
papers?

ANNA : They are forged.

MARTINS : Why?

ANNA : The Russians would claim me. I come from Estonia.[38]
In the open doorway stands the OLD WOMAN. *She does*
not come in.

OLD WOMAN *in German* : The way they behave — breaking
in like this. I am so sorry . . .

---

[37] In the film, the following sequence is added:
MARTINS *to* CALLOWAY : Mind if I use that line in my next Western?
You can't chuck me out, my papers are in order.
PAINE *to* ANNA : Your receipt for the letters, miss.
ANNA : I don't want it.
PAINE : Well, I've got it when you want it, miss.
[38] In the film, ANNA comes from Czechoslovakia.

47

ANNA *takes no notice — the* WOMAN *goes on talking in German to* MARTINS.

MARTINS : What's she say?

ANNA : Only complaining about the way they behave — it's her house.

MARTINS *looking around* : Is it . . .

ANNA : Give her some cigarettes.

> MARTINS *gives her four cigarettes, which she will not at first accept, but finally does so with great grace.* MARTINS *goes back to* ANNA.

CALLOWAY : Ready, Miss Schmidt?

MARTINS : Don't be scared. If I can only clear up this mess about Harry — you'll be okay.

ANNA *glancing up at the picture* : Sometimes he said I laughed too much. *To* CALLOWAY. Yes.

MARTINS : What was that doctor's name?

ANNA *spelling it* : Winkel.

CALLOWAY : What do you want to see a doctor for?

> MARTINS *touches his mouth where* PAINE *hit him.*

MARTINS : [About my mouth.]³⁹

> *The* OLD WOMAN *watches them downstairs. Dissolve.*

38. DR. WINKEL'S FLAT. DINING ROOM (NIGHT):
> *A chicken being carefully dissected. The bell rings.*

39. DR. WINKEL'S FLAT. PASSAGE (NIGHT):
> *A* MAID *passes along and opens the door.* MARTINS *stands outside.*

MARTINS : Is Dr. Winkel in?

MAID : Die Sprechstund ist von drei bis fünf. (His consulting hours are 3 till 5.)

> *She prepares to close the door.*

MARTINS : I want Dr. Winkel. Don't you speak any English?

MAID : Nein.

MARTINS : Dr. Winkel, I . . . *He points at himself* . . . want to see Dr. Winkel. Tell him a friend of Harry Lime.

---

³⁹ In the film, MARTINS says: 'A bruised lip.' This scene is followed by Scene 42.
> INTERNATIONAL POLICE HEADQUARTERS (NIGHT):
> > ANNA'S *letters are being gone through in detail and photographed.*

40. DR. WINKEL'S DINING ROOM (NIGHT):
We cut back to the hands carving the chicken. They suddenly stay still. The knife is put down. A voice calls out something in German.

VOICE *in German*: Show him into the waiting-room, Hilda.

41. DR. WINKEL'S WAITING-ROOM (NIGHT):
The MAID *shows* MARTINS *into the waiting-room and leaves him there.* DR. WINKEL'S *waiting-room reminds one of an antique shop that specialises in religious objets d'art. There are more crucifixes hanging on the walls and perched on the cupboards and occasional tables than one can count, none of later date than the seventeenth century. There are statues in wood and ivory. There are a number of reliquaries: little bits of bone marked with saints' names and set in oval frames on a background of tinfoil. Even the high-backed, hideous chairs look as if they had been sat in by cardinals. Through the open doorway can be seen the stick with the ivory top that* KURTZ *was carrying earlier. A sneeze disturbs him.*

DR. WINKEL *is very small, neat, very clean, in a black tail-coat and a high stiff collar; his little black moustache is like an evening tie. He sneezes again. Perhaps he is cold because he is so clean.*

WINKEL: [Mr. Martins?][40]

MARTINS: Dr. Winkel?
MARTINS always pronounces this name wrong, as though it were the name of the shellfish, so that the ' W ' is pronounced like an English ' W ' and not as in German as a ' V '. This annoys WINKEL.

WINKEL: Vinkel.
When he bows there is a very slight creak as though his shirt front is celluloid. Or does he wear stays?

MARTINS: You have an interesting collection here.

WINKEL: Yes.

[MARTINS: These saints' bones . . .

WINKEL: The bones of chickens.
MARTINS *pauses by yet another crucifix, the figure*

---

[40] In the film, DR. WINKEL says good evening in German.

49

hanging with arms above the head: a face of elongated El Greco agony.

MARTINS : That's a strange crucifix.

WINKEL : Jansenist.

MARTINS : Never heard the word. Why are the arms above the head?

WINKEL : Because he died, in their view, only for the elect.

DR. WINKEL *takes a large white handkerchief out of his sleeve rather as though he were a conjuror producing his country's flag, and blows his nose neatly and thoroughly twice, closing each nostril in turn. One expects him to throw away the handkerchief after one use.*][41]

WINKEL : Would you mind, Mr. Martins, coming to the point? I have guests waiting.

MARTINS : You and I were both friends of Harry Lime.

WINKEL *unyieldingly* : I was his medical adviser.

MARTINS : I want to find out all I can.

WINKEL : Find out?

MARTINS : Hear the details.

WINKEL : I can tell you very little. He was knocked over by a car. He was dead when I arrived.

MARTINS : Who was there?

WINKEL : Two friends of his.

MARTINS : You're sure . . . Two?

WINKEL : Quite sure.

MARTINS : Would he have been conscious at all?

WINKEL : I understand he was . . . yes . . . for a short time . . . while they carried him into the house.

MARTINS : In great pain?

WINKEL : Not necessarily.

MARTINS : Would he have been capable of . . . well, making plans to look after me and others? In those few moments?

WINKEL *looks at the nails on one hand.*

WINKEL : I cannot give an opinion. I was not there.

---

[41] In the film, the following sequence is seen:

A small and disgusting little dog barks and WINKEL *marshals it out of the room with a great rigmarole in German.*

MARTIN : That your dog?

WINKEL : Yes.

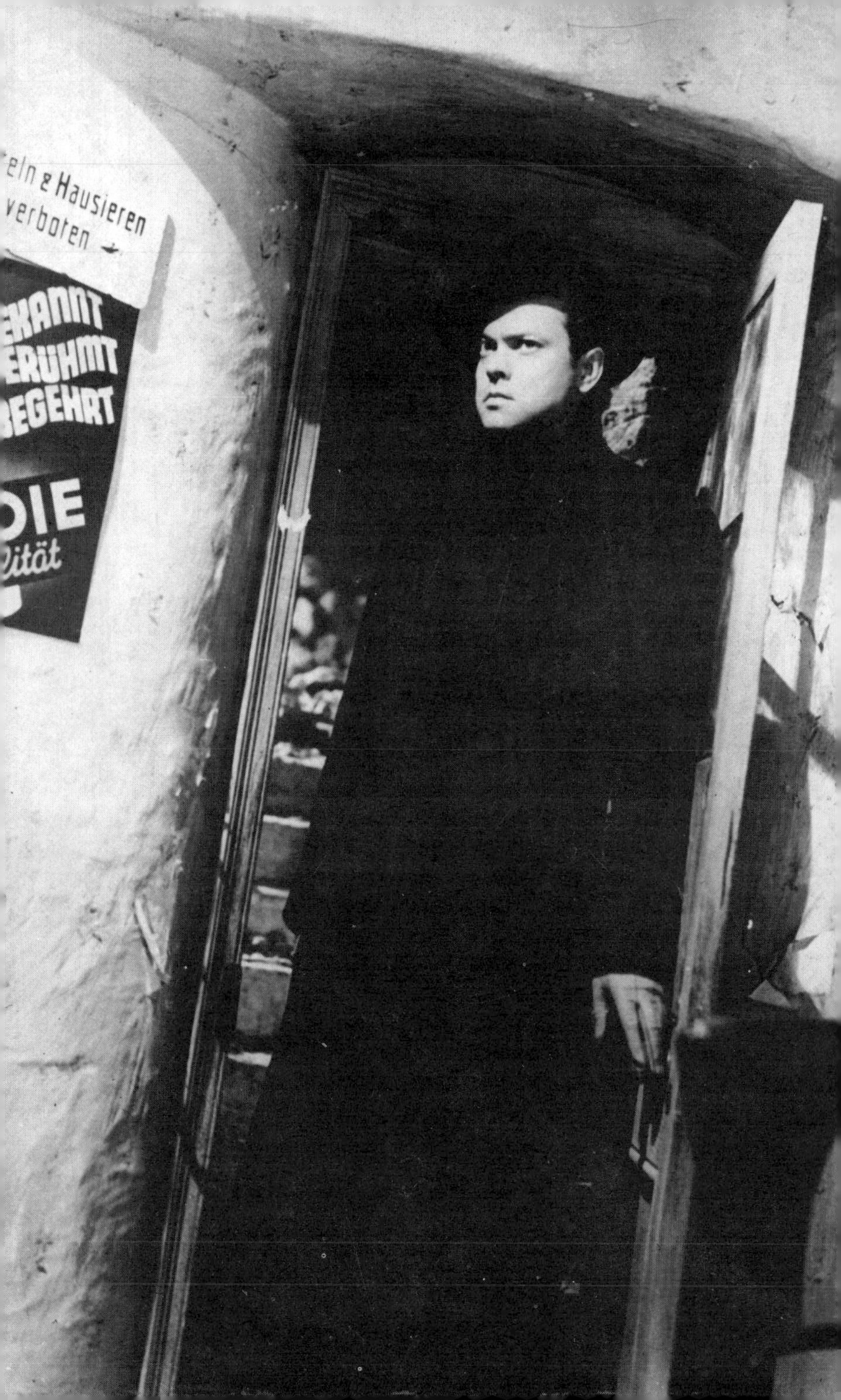
Hausieren
verboten
BEGEHRT
DIE

[DR. WINKEL *takes a silver pencil out of his pocket and cleans one nail with the point.*][42]

WINKEL : My opinion is limited to the causes of death. Have you any reason to be dissatisfied?

MARTINS : Could his death have been . . . not accidental?

DR. WINKEL *puts out a hand and straightens a crucifix on the wall, and flicks some imaginary dust off the feet.*

MARTINS *trying to make himself clear* : Could it have been . . .

WINKEL : Yes?

MARTINS : Could he have been pushed, Dr. Winkel?

WINKEL *stonily correcting him* : Vinkel, Vinkel.

DR. WINKEL *is a very cautious doctor. His statements are so limited that you cannot for a moment doubt their veracity.*

WINKEL : I cannot give an opinion. The injuries to the head and skull would have been the same.

Dissolve.

43. CALLOWAY'S OFFICE (NIGHT):

[CALLOWAY *sits at his desk with* ANNA *before him. On his desk, a bundle of letters.*][43]

CALLOWAY : I can let you have these back, Miss Schmidt. Will you look through, see that they are right, and sign the receipt?

He pushes the receipt across to her, watching her closely.

ANNA : But my passport?

CALLOWAY : We need that for a while longer.

[ANNA *begins to count the letters. The door opens and a Russian Officer,* BRODSKY, *enters.*

---

42 In the film, WINKEL studies a statuette.
43 In the film, the scene begins with the following sequence:

ANNA *paces up and down* CALLOWAY'S *office.* CALLOWAY *enters, but is called back by a Russian Officer,* BRODSKY.

BRODSKY : Major, major, could I see you for a moment, please?

CALLOWAY : Certainly, Brodsky. What is it?

BRODSKY : These forgeries, very clever . . . we too are interested in this case. Have you arrested the girl? Please, keep this passport to yourself until I make some enquiries, will you, major?

CALLOWAY : Yes, of course.

BRODSKY : Thank you.

CALLOWAY *re-enters his office and indicates* ANNA'S *letters on his desk.*

BRODSKY: I've brought the passport back. Very cleverly done. *He drops the passport on the desk.* You know we are interested in this case. Have you arrested the girl? *He takes a long look at* ANNA.

CALLOWAY: Not yet.

BRODSKY: You'll remember we have a claim to the body. See you tonight, Calloway. *He goes out.*]

ANNA *with fear*: What did he mean?

CALLOWAY: You know as much as I do.

[ANNA: There is a letter missing.

CALLOWAY: Yes.

ANNA: Why did you keep it?

CALLOWAY: To have a photostat made.

> CALLOWAY, *to prevent himself embarrassing* ANNA, *goes to the window and speaks his next line with his back turned.*]

CALLOWAY: Miss Schmidt, you were intimate with Lime, weren't you?

ANNA: We loved each other. Do you mean that?

> CALLOWAY *is looking through the window.*

[44. STREET. LOCATION (NIGHT):

> MARTINS *is waiting on the other side of the road. We see him from* CALLOWAY'S *viewpoint.*]

45. CALLOWAY'S OFFICE (NIGHT):

CALLOWAY *turning from the window and picking a photograph from the desk*: Know this man?

ANNA *after a quick look at the photograph*: I've never seen him.

CALLOWAY: But you've heard of him — Joseph Harbin. [A medical orderly.][44]

ANNA: No.

CALLOWAY: It's stupid to lie to me, Miss Schmidt. I am in a position to help you.

ANNA: I am not lying. You are wrong about Harry. You are wrong about everything.

CALLOWAY: In the letter we've kept, Lime asked you to telephone a good friend of his called Joseph. He gave you the

---

[44] In the film, CALLOWAY says: ' He works in a military hospital.'

number . . . [It's the number of the hospital where Harbin worked.]⁴⁵

ANNA: Oh, that. Yes, I remember that. It wasn't important.

CALLOWAY: What was the message?

ANNA: [I can't remember.]⁴⁶

CALLOWAY: Harbin disappeared the day you telephoned — I want to find him. *He picks up the passport and turns it over in his hands.* You can help us.

ANNA: What can I tell you but . . . CALLOWAY *looks up.* You've got everything upside down. CALLOWAY *gets up.*

CALLOWAY: Right, Miss Schmidt. We'll send for you when we want you. That friend of yours is waiting for you — a rather troublesome fellow.

Dissolve.

46. THE CASANOVA CLUB (NIGHT):
A dance floor with tables round it; up a short flight of stairs, a bar and cloakroom. KURTZ, *playing a violin with two other players, is going from table to table. As he passes one table, we see* CARTER *and* TOMBS. *They go up the stairs to the bar and cloakroom. As they reach the cloakroom, the street door opens and* MARTINS *and* ANNA *enter.* ANNA *goes up to the bar.* CARTER *sees* MARTINS *as he turns, struggling to get into his overcoat.*

CARTER: Hello, Mr. Martins. Goodness, I'm glad I ran into you.

MARTINS: Good evening.

CARTER: I've been looking all over town for you, Mr. Martins. [I've arranged a lecture at Innsbruck.

MARTINS: You what?

TOMBS *gloomily*: Wait till you hear the subject.]⁴⁷

CARTER: They want you to talk on the Crisis of Faith.

---

⁴⁵ In the film, CALLOWAY adds: '. . . of the Casanova Club, that's where a lot of friends of Lime used to go.'

⁴⁶ In the film, ANNA adds: 'Something about meeting Harry at his home.'

⁴⁷ In the film, the following sequence is played:
CRABBIT: I've arranged that lecture for tomorrow.
MARTINS: What about?
CRABBIT: On the modern novel, you remember what we arranged.

MARTINS : What does that mean?

TOMBS : We thought you'd know. You're a writer, old chap.

CARTER : We'll talk again after the discussion. I'll let you know the time.

[MARTIN : What discussion?

CARTER : The lecture on the modern novel. You remember — what we arranged at the hotel.

MARTINS : Oh yes, that's right.

TOMBS : So long, old man.]

ANNA *is at the bar.* MARTINS *comes up.*

MARTINS : Drink?

He takes out his army money.

ANNA : And they won't take that stuff here. *To* BARMAN. Two whiskies. *She opens her bag.*

MARTINS *turning round on his stool sees* KURTZ *playing at a table below, where a fat woman is sitting with an elderly man. He is pouring it out with great emotion — eyes slit and swimming, his shoulders move with the slow rhythm and his head nods with appreciation.* MARTINS *watches him with suspicion.* KURTZ *has not yet seen him.*

ANNA : Your whisky.

He half-turns back to the bar. ANNA, *who has turned her bag out, is putting her change back. She picks up a snapshot and is about to put it back in her bag.*

MARTINS : Harry?

She gives it to him — they stare at it together.

ANNA : He moved his head, but the rest is good.

KURTZ *is playing from table to table, followed by a double bass and second violin — sees* MARTINS *and* ANNA *— leaves the others and moves to the bar. He seems completely unperturbed and comes up the stairs to the bar. He bows to* ANNA.

KURTZ : Miss Schmidt. You've found out my little secret. A man must live. *To* MARTINS. How goes the investigation? Have you proved the policeman wrong?

MARTINS : [Yes.][48]

---

[48] In the film, MARTINS says: ' Not yet.'

KURTZ, *who is aware he has carried off a tricky situation well, has been a little over-exhilarated, but this plain statement damps him.*

KURTZ : Our friend Winkel said you had called. Perhaps he was helpful? *He cannot avoid a shade of anxiety.*

MARTINS : No.

KURTZ : Mr. Tyler is here tonight.

MARTINS : I thought he left Vienna.

KURTZ : He's back now.

MARTINS : I want to meet all Harry's friends.

KURTZ : I'll bring him to you.

KURTZ *goes back to the dance floor.*

ANNA : Haven't you done enough today? *She is worn out with reminders of* HARRY.

MARTINS : That porter said three men carried the body, and two of them are here.

MARTINS *turns from the bar and sees* TYLER: *a man with tousled grey hair, a worried, kindly, humanitarian face and long-sighted eyes.*

KURTZ : Mr. Tyler, Mr. Martins.

TYLER : Any friend of Harry is a friend of mine.

KURTZ : I'll leave you together. *He goes.*

TYLER : Good evening, Miss Schmidt. You remember me?

ANNA : Yes. *The memory is obviously not pleasant.*

TYLER : I helped Harry fix her papers, Mr. Martins. Not the sort of thing I should confess to a stranger, but you have to break the rules sometimes. Humanity's a duty. Cigarette, Miss Schmidt? Keep the pack.

MARTINS *is growing impatient with all this talk.*

MARTINS : [I want to hear about Harry's death.][49]

ANNA SCHMIDT *takes her glass and moves away down the bar. She cannot bear any more of this. She sits there, during the ensuing scene, smoking cigarette after cigarette.*

TYLER *to* BARMAN : Two large whiskies and a small one for the lady. *To* MARTINS. It was a terrible thing. I was just crossing the road to go to Harry. He and the Baron were on the sidewalk.

---

[49] In the film, MARTINS says: ' I understand you were with Harry . . .'

MARTINS'S *eyes go to* KURTZ *who has come into sight below, playing at a table as before. He glances towards* MARTINS *and nods at him with a smile.*

TYLER : Maybe if I hadn't started across the road, it wouldn't have happened. I can't help blaming myself and wishing things had been different. Anyway he saw me and stepped off the sidewalk to meet me, and the truck . . . it was terrible. Mr. Martins, terrible. *He swallows his whisky.* I've never seen a man killed before.

MARTINS : There was something wrong about Harry's death.

TYLER : Of course, there was. [Two more whiskies.]

MARTINS : You think so too?

TYLER : It was so damned stupid for a man like Harry to be killed in a [piddling] street accident.

MARTINS : That's all you meant?

TYLER : What else?

MARTINS : Who was the third man?

TYLER *takes up his glass.*

TYLER : I oughtn't to drink it. It makes me acid. What man would you be referring to, Mr. Martins?

MARTINS : I was told a third man helped you and Kurtz with the body.

TYLER : I don't know how you got that idea. You'll find all about it in the Inquest report. There was just the two of us. Me and the Baron. Who could have told you a story like that?

MARTINS: I was talking to the porter at Harry's place. He was cleaning the window and looked out.

TYLER *with great calm* : And saw the accident?

MARTINS : No. Three men carrying the body, that's all.

TYLER : Why wasn't he at the Inquest?

MARTINS : He didn't want to get involved.

TYLER: You'll never teach these Austrians to be good citizens. It was his duty to give the evidence, even though he remembered wrong. What else did he tell you?

MARTINS : That Harry was dead when he was carried into the house. Somebody's lying.

TYLER : Not necessarily. [It's an odd thing, Mr. Martins, with accidents. You'll never get two reports that coincide. Why, even the Baron and I disagreed about details. The thing happens so suddenly, you aren't prepared to notice things.]

MARTINS *watching the other man's reactions* : The police say Harry was mixed up in some racket.

TYLER : That's quite impossible. He had a great sense of duty.

MARTINS : Kurtz seemed to think it was possible.

TYLER : The Baron doesn't understand how an Anglo-Saxon feels.[50]

He looks across at ANNA *and finishes his drink. [He speaks as he rises.]*

TYLER : That's a nice girl, that. But she ought to be careful in Vienna. Everybody ought to be careful in a city like this. *Dissolve.*

[47. ANNA'S ROOM (NIGHT) :

ANNA *lies awake in bed, with her arms behind her head, staring at the ceiling. The street lamps outside cast shifting shadows on the ceiling, and something goes tap, tap, tap.* ANNA *looks in the direction of the sound and sees what it is — the cord of the window shade hitting the back of* HARRY's *photograph. She puts out her hand and lays the photograph face down.*

48. STREET. LOCATION (DAWN) :

International Patrol car passes along empty streets. In the background is one lighted window — the silhouette of a figure is seen telephoning.

49. TYLER'S ROOM. LOCATION (DAWN) :

TYLER *is putting down the receiver of his telephone. He opens a drawer and takes out two packets of American cigarettes, looks in a mirror, carefully rumples his hair and makes for the door.*

50. WINKEL'S FRONT DOOR. LOCATION (DAWN):

DR. WINKEL, *dressed as always very neatly, comes out of his door, carrying a briefcase. He trots down the stairs, expressionless, giving nothing away.*

---

[50] In the film, the following dialogue is added :
MARTINS : He seems to have been around a bit. Do you know a man called Harbin . . . Joseph Harbin?
POPESCU : No.

51. KURTZ'S FLAT: EXTERIOR. LOCATION (DAWN):
Through the open front door we see KURTZ *adjusting his toupée. He walks down the street.*

52. VIENNA EXTERIOR. LOCATION (DAWN):
Dawn over the canal and the ruined quays: the Russian zone notice: the Prater with the idle wheel: the Danube. KURTZ *walks through these scenes.*][51]

53. REICHSBRUCKE: EXTERIOR. LOCATION (DAWN):
A man with his back turned to the camera waits on the bridge. He is joined one after the other by TYLER KURTZ *and* WINKEL. *They talk together out of hearing.*

[54. ANNA'S ROOM (MORNING):
ANNA *is at last asleep. Dissolve.*

55. STREET: EXTERIOR. LOCATION (DAY):
In the centre of the dissolve there is the sound of a crash which continues into this scene. A tram is stopping suddenly with a jerk. MARTINS *is seen from the rear getting out; he walks towards the Public Library. Dissolve.*

56. PUBLIC LIBRARY: INTERIOR. LOCATION (DAY):
Official is finishing his translation of the Inquest report to MARTINS. *He has been making endless notes and has obviously spent some time here.*

OFFICIAL *in a broken accent*: . . . exonerated the driver and brought in a verdict of accidental death.]
Dissolve.

---

[51] In the film, four shots replace Scenes 47 to 52.
A. POPESCU'S ROOM (DAWN):
POPESCU *is finishing a telephone call.*
POPESCU: He will meet us at the bridge, good.
Dissolve.
B. KURTZ'S HOUSE: EXTERIOR (DAWN):
KURTZ *leaves his house surreptitiously. Dissolve.*
C. WINKEL'S HOUSE: EXTERIOR (DAWN):
WINKEL *wheels out an old bicycle and rides away. Dissolve.*
D. POPESCU'S FRONT DOOR (DAWN):
POPESCU, *dressed in an overcoat, steps out. Dissolve.*

57. HARRY'S FLAT : EXTERIOR. LOCATION (DAY):
Martins is pacing out the distance from the door to the point where Harry was killed, and various other distances. Then he paces back along the pavement where the body was carried, and looks up to the window of Harry's flat, from which the Porter had seen the third man. Staring down at him is the Porter, duster in hand.
Porter *calling softly down* : Mein Herr.
Martins : Yes?
Porter : I am not a bad man, mein Herr. Not a bad man. Is it really so important?
Martins : Very important.
Porter : Come this evening when my wife is out then.
Martins : I'll come, but tell me now. Was the car . . .
Porter : Shsh. *He slams the window.*

58. HARRY'S FLAT (DAY):
The Porter slams the window and turns towards camera. He stays still, listening. The sound of squeaking shoes approaching from the next room. As they come close, there is a look of horror on the Porter's face.
Dissolve.

59. ANNA'S ROOM (DAY):
The grey early-evening time before it is quite dark enough to switch on the lights. Anna is standing by the table on which are the roneo-ed sheets of a play. She has been trying to learn a new part. She turns and the camera turns with her to pick up Martins in the doorway, in a wet mackintosh. For a moment, because her mind is in the past, she almost thinks it is Harry. She makes a motion towards him and then turns away.

Anna: Come in. [I can't give you a drink. Except tea. There's some of that packet left.
Martins : No, thank you. You know I can't stand tea. *He sits down on the divan.* I'm feeling cross-eyed — been looking at Inquest Reports — Police Reports — but I finally got something.] The porter's going to talk to us tonight.
Anna : Need we go through it all again?
Martins : I can manage alone. *He picks up the play.* Busy?
Anna : Another part I've got to learn.

MARTINS : Shall I hear you?

ANNA *sceptically* : In German?

MARTINS : I can try. Tragedy or comedy?

ANNA : Comedy. I'm not the right shape for tragedy.

> *She hands him the part and shows him the cue, which he ludicrously mispronounces. They go on for a few lines, but she is obviously getting them wrong.*

ANNA : It's no good.

MARTINS : One of the bad days?

ANNA : It's always bad about this time. He used to look in round six. I've been frightened, I've been alone, I've been without friends and money, but I've never known anything like this.

> *ANNA plonks herself down on a hard chair opposite him. It is as if she had been fighting for days not to say this, and now surrenders.*

ANNA: Please talk. Tell me about him; tell me about the Harry you knew.

> *MARTINS takes a long look at her. All the grace she may have had seems to have been folded up with her dresses and put away for professional use. This ANNA is for every-day. Suddenly it is he who is less willing to talk of HARRY.*

MARTINS : What kind of things?

ANNA : Anything. Just talk. Where did you see him last? When? What did you do?

MARTINS : We drank too much. We quarrelled. I thought he was making a pass at my girl.

ANNA : Where's she?

MARTINS : I don't know. That was nine years ago.

ANNA: Tell me more. (Still on page 51)

MARTINS : It's difficult. You knew Harry; we didn't do anything terribly amusing — he just made it all seem such fun.

ANNA : I know a little what you mean. Was he clever when he was a boy?

> *He gets up restlessly and looks out of the window.*

MARTINS : I suppose so. He could fix anything.

ANNA : Tell me.

MARTINS : Oh, little things — how to put up your temperature before an exam — the best crib — how to avoid this and that.

ANNA : He fixed my papers for me. He heard the Russians were repatriating people like me who came from Estonia. He knew the right man straight away for forging stamps.

MARTINS : When he was only fourteen, he taught me the three card trick. That was growing up fast.

ANNA : He never grew up. The world grew up round him, that's all — and buried him.

> [*She begins to cry quietly, and* MARTINS *suddenly turns from the window.*

MARTINS : He's dead. You can't go on remembering him for ever.

ANNA : Something may happen.

MARTINS : What do you mean?

ANNA : Perhaps there'll be another war or I'll die or the Russians will take me.

MARTINS : Anna, life goes on. It'll get better.] You'll fall in love again.

> ANNA *turns to the sink with the remains of a dinner.*

ANNA : Don't you see I don't want to. I don't ever want to.

> MARTINS *moving away from the window, passes her and sympathetically scratches the top of her head.*

MARTINS : Come out and have a drink.

> ANNA *looks quickly up.*

ANNA : Why did you say that?

MARTINS : It seemed like a good idea.

ANNA : It was just what he used to say. [And when I said ' I've got to be at the theatre ', he'd say . . .

MARTINS : ' Time for a quick one '][52]

> *They laugh a moment.*

ANNA : If we've got to see the porter, we'd better go . . .

> *She picks up her part and starts for the door.*

MARTINS : I thought you didn't want . . .

ANNA : We're both in it, Harry.

MARTINS : My name's Rollo.

ANNA : I'm sorry.

MARTINS : You needn't be. [I'm bad at names too. Ask

---

52 In the film, MARTINS says: ' Well, I didn't learn that from him.'

Callaghan.][53]

In the doorway she turns and speaks with the first real friendliness.

[ANNA : What fun we all might have had, him and you and me.

MARTINS : As long as I kept off the extra glass.]

ANNA : You know, you ought to find yourself a girl.

Dissolve.

60. HARRY'S STREET. PART LOCATION (NIGHT):
As ANNA *and* MARTINS *walk along the street, lights go on. At the end of the road a group of people are gathered in spite of thin icy rain. The lights are reflected in the puddles.* ANNA *is staring down the road with some uneasiness, trying to make out what is happening.*

MARTINS : Isn't that Harry's? [It looks like a wedding.

ANNA : At this time of day?

She walks more slowly. The crowd makes her uneasy.

MARTINS : A demonstration?

ANNA : They don't allow demonstrations.] *She stops altogether.* Let's go away.

MARTINS : Stay here. I'll see what it's about.

MARTINS *walks slowly on alone. It is not a political meeting, for no one is making a speech. Heads turn to watch him come, as though he is somebody expected.* MARTINS *reaches the fringe of the little crowd and speaks to a* MAN *there.*

MARTINS *trying out some bad German* : Was ist? *He waves his hand at the crowd.*

MAN : They wait to see him brought out.

MARTINS : Who?

MAN : The porter.

MARTINS : What's he done?

MAN : Nobody knows yet. They can't make their minds up in there — it might be suicide, you see, but why should he have cut his own throat . . .?

The small child, called HANSL, *whom* MARTINS *saw on his visit to* HARRY'S *flat, comes up to his informant and pulls at his hand.*

---

[53] In the film, MARTINS says : 'You might get my name right.'

66

HANSL: Papa, papa.

His face is pinched and blue with cold and more unpleasant than ever.

HANSL *in German*: Papa, I heard the big man say, ' Can you tell me what the foreigner looked like? '

MAN *to* MARTINS: Ha. He had a row with a foreigner, they think he did it . . .

HANSL: Papa, papa.

MAN: Ja, Hansl?

HANSL: Wie ich durch's Gitter geschaut habe, hab'ich Blut auf'm Koks gesehen. (When I looked through the grating, I could see some blood on the coke.)

MAN *admiringly to* MARTINS: What imagination! He thought when he looked through the grating, he could see blood on the coke.

The child stares solemnly up at MARTINS.

HANSL: Papa.

MAN: Ja, Hansl?

HANSL *in German*: Das ist der Fremde. (That's the foreigner.)

The MAN *gives a big laugh that causes a dozen heads to turn.*

MAN: Listen to him, sir. He thinks you did it because you are a foreigner. There are more foreigners here these days than Viennese.

HANSL: Papa, papa.

MAN: Yes, Hansl?

HANSL points. A knot of police surrounds the covered stretcher which they lower down the steps. The PORTER'S *wife comes out at the tail of the procession; she has a shawl over her head and an old sackcloth coat. Somebody gives her a hand and she looks round with a lost, hopeless gaze at this crowd of strangers. If there are friends there, she does not recognise them, looking from face to face. To avoid her look,* MARTINS *bends to do up his shoelace, but kneeling there, he finds himself on a level with* HANSL'S *scrutinising gaze. Walking back up the street towards* ANNA, MARTINS *looks behind him once. The child is pulling at his father's hand, and he can see the lips forming round those syllables, ' Papa, papa '.*

67

MARTINS : The porter's been murdered. Let's get away from here. They're asking about the foreigner who called on him.

They hurry away. Unknown to them, they are followed at a distance by little HANSL, *who drags his father after him.* ANNA *and* MARTINS *walk as naturally as they can, but sometimes hurrying too much, and then slowing too much.*[54]

ANNA : Then what he said was true. There *was* a third man.

MARTINS *does not reply. The tram-cars flash like icicles at the end of the street.* MARTINS *turns round and sees* HANSL *and his father following with a few of the men who were outside the* PORTER'S *doorway.*

MARTINS : Anna. *He indicates their pursuers.*

ANNA : That child?

MARTINS *nods. They hurry round the corner.*

61. CINEMA. LOCATION (NIGHT):
Outside a cinema a small queue is just moving in.

MARTINS : Come in here.

ANNA *takes money from her bag, and they buy tickets. They go into the dark cinema.*

62. CINEMA. INTERIOR. LOCATION (NIGHT):
The film which is being shown is a well-known Hope-Crosby-Lamour film with voices dubbed in German. Big laughs come from the audience. Crosby begins to sing in German.

ANNA : Be careful. The porter knew so little and they murdered him. You know as much . . .

MARTINS : You can't be careful of someone you don't know.

The camera takes in the anonymous, shadowy faces sitting round them.

MARTINS : Go on to the theatre. I'd better not come near you again till this is fixed. ANNA *gets up.*

ANNA : What are you going to do?

MARTINS *with harassed bewilderment*: I wish I knew. *He looks back at the screen.*

ANNA : Be sensible. Tell Colonel Calloway. *Dissolve.*

[63. SACHER'S HOTEL. LOCATION (NIGHT):

---

[54] In the film, this scene is shot in a very much shortened version, and far more visually.

MARTINS *hurries up — a taxi is waiting outside the Hotel — MARTINS is about to get in, but there is no driver — he turns into the hotel.*]

64. SACHER'S RECEPTION DESK (NIGHT):
A MAN, with a chauffeur's cap and a shifty expression, is just leaving the desk as MARTINS comes hurriedly in. The MAN turns and stares at him as he passes. MARTINS'S mind is made up.

MARTINS *to* PORTER : Get Colonel Callaghan on the 'phone.

PORTER : I don't know him, sir.

MARTINS : Calloway then. I don't care what his name is. Get him quickly. It's urgent.

PORTER : Do you know his number, sir?

MARTINS : Of course, I don't. Is there a car I can use?

PORTER : There's one right here for you, sir.

MARTINS : Fine.

He strides out, followed by a sub-porter.

[*The* PORTER *calls after him.*

PORTER : Captain Carter has been on the 'phone to you, sir. He was anxious to speak to you. About a lecture . . .

MARTINS : Tell him he can put his damned culture in the dustbin.]

65. SACHER'S HOTEL. LOCATION (NIGHT):
The sub-porter opens the door of a car driven by the shifty MAN in the chauffeur's cap.

66. CAR. BACK PROJECTION (NIGHT):
As MARTINS sits down, the car immediately begins to move off.

MARTINS : International Police Headquarters. Colonel Calloway's Office.

The MAN does not reply and the car gathers speed. It plunges into ill-lit streets. MARTINS peers anxiously out.

67. CAR. STREET. LOCATION (NIGHT):
The taxi speeds around a corner — it almost mounts the kerb — it is driving to a more deserted part of the city.

68. CAR. BACK PROJECTION (NIGHT):
MARTINS : Slower. Slower.[55] *The* DRIVER *pays no attention.*

---

[55] In the film, MARTINS adds: 'You don't know where to take me yet.'

This isn't the way to the International Police. Where are we going?

The DRIVER *turns his head and speaks in German, with a malevolent ring.* MARTINS *makes a joke which sounds hollow to his own ears . . .*

MARTINS : Have you got orders to kill me?

DRIVER : Ich kann nicht Englisch. (I do not speak English.)

69. CULTURAL CENTRE. LOCATION (NIGHT) :

The car pulls through the open gates of a courtyard and drives around to the rear of a house, stopping with a jerk alongside a big doorway. The DRIVER *opens the door.*

DRIVER : Bitte. (Please.)

MARTINS : This isn't police headquarters.

DRIVER : Bitte.

The DRIVER *puts his hand into the car to help* MARTINS *out, and* MARTINS *shakes it off.*

DRIVER : Bitte.

The DRIVER *turns towards the big doors and starts to push them open.* MARTINS *edges out of the car and turns to try to escape, but the car blocks his way. The light from the now open doorway falls across him.*

VOICE : Oh, Mr. Martins.

He looks up startled.

70. CULTURAL CENTRE . HALLWAY (NIGHT :

Bright lights shine out. MARTINS *sees* CARTER *advancing through a throng of women.*

CARTER : Better late than never. *He draws* MARTINS *inside.*

71. CULTURAL CENTRE. RECEPTION AND ANTE-ROOM (NIGHT) :

Hemmed in by CARTER *and* TOMBS *and the attendant women,* MARTINS *is hustled like a Führer through the anteroom which is being used as a cloakroom. His mackintosh is drawn off him as he walks. In the large inner room where the discussion will be held, the uncomfortable chairs are arranged in rows; a buffet has been set up laden with nothing more exhilarating than cocoa; an urn steams; a woman's face is shiny with exertion; and huddled in the background, like faces in a family album, the earnest and dreary features of constant readers.* MARTINS *looks behind him, but the door has closed. There is no escape.*

[MARTINS *desperately to* CARTER: I'm sorry, but . . .

CARTER: For goodness sake, do your stuff, old man. The Brigadier's here.

Three chairs for CARTER, TOMBS *and* MARTINS *face the others.*

CARTER *in an undertone to* TOMBS: You give them the works?

TOMBS: Oh no. This is your funeral, old man.

CARTER: Well, you read one of his books, didn't you?

TOMBS: Nothing doing.

CARTER *knocks on the table, and as he begins to speak, people drift to their seats. The* BRIGADIER *listens and hangs on every word.*]

CARTER: Ladies and Gentlemen, we have with us tonight Mr. Rollo Martins, one of the great writers from the other side. Here he is. We've all of us read his books. Wonderful stuff. Literature depends on character — I've read that somewhere — and Mr. Martins's characters — well, there's nothing quite like them, is there? You know what I mean. We ought to give him a great welcome.

The faces of the listeners watch with avid expectancy; one figure jumps up to ask a question. Dissolve.[56]

72. RECEPTION ROOM (NIGHT):

It is some time later and MARTINS *already looks harried and confused by the questions.* CARTER *is worried,* [*and* TOMBS *sits in despair — with one eye on the* BRIGADIER.]

AUSTRIAN WOMAN: Do you believe in the stream of consciousness?

MARTINS *to* CARTER: Stream of what?

CARTER gives a gesture of despair.

[73. STAIRCASE (NIGHT):

A bowed figure slowly mounts the stairs towards the

---

[56] In the film, the dissolve was to:
POPESCU ON THE TELEPHONE. INTERIOR (NIGHT):
POPESCU: . . . Bring the car and anyone else who would like to come. Don't be long . . . *Dissolve.*

71

double doors. It is dark on the stairs and we cannot make out the face. By now we are prepared to see in all strangers, in all mysterious figures, the possible features of the third man.

74. RECEPTION ROOM (NIGHT):
We can see, though MARTINS *cannot, right through the anteroom to the door. Somebody opens the door and the figure from the stairs comes in. We still do not see the face.*

AUSTRIAN YOUNG MAN *with rather an effeminate manner*: Among the great English poets, where would you put Oscar Wilde?

MARTINS: What do you mean, put? I don't want to put anybody anywhere.][57]

TYLER: Can I ask Mr. Martins if he's engaged on a new book?

MARTINS, CARTER [*and* TOMBS] *look at the doorway.* TYLER *stands there.* MARTINS *takes him in for a moment in silence. He recognises the challenge.*

MARTINS: Yes . . . yes . . . It's called ' The Third Man '.

WOMAN: A novel, Mr. Martins?

MARTINS: It's founded on fact.

[CARTER: I'm so glad you were able to come, Mr. Tyler. *To* MARTINS. Mr. Tyler is here on a cultural mission.][58]

---

[57] In the film, the following adaptation of the later part of the screen-play appears here:
Two ladies leave the audience.
MAN IN AUDIENCE: What author has chiefly influenced you?
MARTINS: Gray.
LADY IN AUDIENCE: Grey? Which Grey?
MARTINS: Zane Gray.
CRABBIT: That's Mr. Martins's little joke, of course. As we all know perfectly well, Zane Gray wrote what we call ' Westerns ' — cowboys and baddies.
ANOTHER MAN: This — er — James Joyce now, where would you put him?
POPESCU *has come in and caught* MARTINS'S *attention.*
MARTINS: Would you mind repeating that question?
MAN *viciously*: Where would you put James Joyce — in what category?
[58] In the film, MARTINS adds: ' It's a murder story.' CRABBIT quickly

72

[TYLER : I guess we all have to get together against the common enemy.

MARTINS : Who's that, Mr. Tyler?

TYLER : Ignorance, Mr. Martins. You know the saying — to know all is to forgive all.

MARTINS : You have to know all first.

CARTER *to his assistant* : Get a chair for Mr. Tyler.

TYLER : Just let me squat here on the edge of the buffet, Captain Carter. *He does so.* I've got to push off in a few minutes.

> *A* WOMAN *wearing a meagre bit of rabbit round her throat, asks the question she has been dying to get out all through the last interchange.*

AUSTRIAN WOMAN : Mr. Martins, what author has chiefly influenced you?

MARTINS : Gray.

ELDERLY AUSTRIAN : Grey? What Grey? I do not know the name.

MARTINS : Zane Gray — I don't know any other.

TOMBS : Don't get above their heads, old chap.

AUSTRIAN : He is a great writer?

CARTER : Terrific. Read him myself.

AUSTRIAN YOUNG MAN : And James Joyce, Mr. Martins?

CARTER *to* TOMBS : Joyce?

TOMBS *to* CARTER : Lord Haw Haw. Don't like the way this is going, old man.

MARTINS : I've never heard of him.

TOMBS : Good line, old chap.

> *There is a lot of ill-suppressed discontent in the audience by this time. A* YOUNG WOMAN *calls out insultingly.*

YOUNG WOMAN : He wrote *Ulysses.*

MARTINS : I don't read Greek.

TYLER *his voice breaking clearly through the twitters* : Mr. Martins, I'd like a word with you about your new novel.

MARTINS : ' The Third Man '?

TYLER : Yes.

---

interjects : ' I'm so glad you were able to come, Mr. Popescu.' To MARTINS. ' Mr. Popescu is a very great supporter of one of our medical charities.'

The meeting slowly quiets to hear them.]

MARTINS : [It's a murder story.] I've just started it.

TYLER : Are you a slow writer, Mr. Martins?

MARTINS : Pretty quick when I get interested.

TYLER : I'd say you were doing something pretty dangerous this time.

MARTINS : Yes?

TYLER : Mixing fact and fiction, like oil and water.

MARTINS : Should I write it as straight fact?

TYLER : Why no, Mr. Martins. I'd say stick to fiction, straight fiction.

MARTINS : I've gone too far with the book, Mr. Tyler.

TYLER : Haven't you ever scrapped a book, Mr. Martins?

MARTINS : Never.

> TYLER *gets lazily up from the edge of the buffet. He touches the urn with his finger.*[59]

[TYLER : Pretty hot. Do you mind if I use your telephone, Captain Carter.

CARTER : Please go ahead. In the anteroom.

> TYLER *strolls out.*

WOMAN : Do you think there's any future, Mr. Martins, for the historical novel?

75. THE ANTEROOM (NIGHT) :

> TYLER *is at the telephone. While he waits,* TYLER *speaks to the girl who is looking after the coats. People are fetching their coats and going out all the time. Snatches of dissatisfied conversation are going on.*

TYLER : You people are doing a wonderful job.

GIRL : Bitte?

TYLER : Never mind. *Into the telephone.* Oh, hello. Yes, I'm at the Cultural Centre. Our friend's here. Very interesting talk, I thought you might like to meet us. We could have a little party. Bring the car and anyone else who'd like to come. Don't be long. *He puts down the receiver.*

---

[59] In the film, POPESCU says: ' Pity,' as he goes out. Then CRABBIT adds, after everybody has shuffled out in dissatisfaction: ' Well, if there are no more questions for Mr. Martins, I think I can call the meeting officially closed.'

76. RECEPTION ROOM (NIGHT):
MARTINS *is wiping perspiration off his forehead and* TOMBS *is leaning gloomily back in his chair. Half the chairs are empty and several others are leaving.*
MARTINS: I've never heard of him. *Desperately* . . . I don't read many books.
TOMBS *to* CARTER: This is disaster, old man.
CARTER: Mr. Martins has had a trying time since he came to Vienna. If there are no more questions . . .
The meeting breaks up. Those that have not already left stand up to go.
The BRIGADIER *approaches* TOMBS *and* CARTER. *The shadow of the approaching reprimand clouds the two men's faces.* MARTINS *is about to leave.*
BRIGADIER *eyeing* CARTER *and* TOMBS: Good evening, Mr. Martins. Hope you're having a pleasant time in Vienna? Where are you staying?
MARTINS: They've put me up at Sacher's.
A look of uneasiness on the faces of CARTER *and* TOMBS.
BRIGADIER *with a look at* CARTER *and* TOMBS: You're lucky. It's usually reserved for officers. *As* MARTINS *moves away* . . . Good night, Mr. Martins.
CARTER: We understand, sir, Colonel Calloway . . .
BRIGADIER: You fellows come and see me tomorrow. 9.30 in my office. In uniform.
77. FRONT DOOR (NIGHT):
TYLER *is standing there looking down the road expectantly as the people are leaving.*]
78. ANTEROOM (NIGHT):
[MARTINS *is coming through in a hurry and stops as he looks down the few stairs and sees a car drive up, and* TYLER *speaking to the two men who are hurriedly getting out.*] TYLER *speaks quietly to them, and we do not hear what is said, but the three men now stand in the narrow hallway obviously waiting for* MARTINS *to come down. They look up the stairs towards him.* MARTINS *looks above him and sees a narrow staircase that leads along a corridor. He makes a dash for this.* TYLER *and the two men have seen him vanish and start up the stairs.*

79. CORRIDOR (NIGHT):

MARTINS *opens the door at random and shuts it behind him. We can hear the three men go by. The room where he stands is in darkness: a curious moaning sound makes him turn and face whatever room it is. He can see nothing and the sound has stopped. He makes a tiny movement and once more it starts, like an impeded breath. He remains still and the sound dies away. Outside somebody calls.*

TYLER'S VOICE: Mr. Martins . . .

Then a new sound starts. It is like somebody whispering — a long continuous monologue in the darkness.

MARTINS: Is anybody there?

The sound stops again. He can stand no more of it. He takes out his lighter. Footsteps go up and down the stairs. He scrapes and scrapes at his lighter in the dark and something rattles in mid-air like a chain.

MARTINS *with the anger of fear*: Is anybody there?

[*Only the click of metal answers him.* MARTINS *feels for a light switch to his right hand and then to his left. He does not dare to go farther because he can no longer locate his fellow occupant; the whisper, the moaning, the click have all stopped. Then he is afraid that he has lost the door and feels wildly for the knob. He begins to be far less afraid of the police than he is of the darkness. Somebody outside switches on the landing light, and the glow under the door gives* MARTINS *his direction.*] *He turns the light switch, and the eyes of a parrot chained to a perch stare beadily at him. Somebody turns the handle of the door, and* MARTINS *has only just time to turn the key. A hand beats on the door.*

MARTINS *sees an open window behind the parrot. He tries to avoid the parrot, who snaps at him as he squeezes by and wounds his hand.* MARTINS *reaches the window and gets out, just as the door is forced open.*

80. EVADING: STREETS. LOCATION (NIGHT):

These shots show MARTINS *evading his pursuers. He manages to get to International Police Headquarters over bomb-sites.*

81. CALLOWAY'S OFFICE (NIGHT):

MARTINS *sits gloomily in front of* CALLOWAY. *He has bound up his left hand, where the parrot bit him, with a handkerchief.*

CALLOWAY *furious* : I told you to go away, Martins. This isn't Santa Fe, I'm not a sheriff, and you aren't a cowboy . . . You've been wanted for murder, you've been associating with suspicious characters . . .

MARTINS : Put down drunk and disorderly too.

CALLOWAY : I have. What's the matter with your hand?

MARTINS : A parrot bit me.

CALLOWAY *looks sharply up and then lets it go. He rings a bell.* PAINE *enters.*

CALLOWAY : Give me the Harry Lime file, Paine, and better give Mr. Martins a double whisky.

PAINE *very efficiently does both.*

MARTINS : I don't need your drinks, Callaghan.

CALLOWAY : You will. I don't want another murder in this case, and you were born to be murdered, so you're going to hear the facts.

MARTINS : You haven't told me a single one yet.

CALLOWAY : You're going to hear plenty now. I suppose you've heard of penicillin.

MARTINS : Well?

CALLOWAY : In Vienna there hasn't been enough penicillin to go round. So a nice trade started here. Stealing penicillin from the military hospitals, diluting it to make it go further, selling it to patients. Do you see what that means?

MARTINS : So you're too busy chasing a few tubes of penicillin to investigate a murder.

CALLOWAY : These *were* murders. Men with gangrened legs, women in childbirth. And there were children too. They used some of this diluted penicillin against meningitis. The lucky children died, the unlucky ones went off their heads. You can see them now in the mental ward. That was the racket Harry Lime organized.

MARTINS : Callaghan, you haven't shown me one shred of evidence.

CALLOWAY : We're coming to that. *He crosses and pulls a*

curtain over the window. A magic lantern show, Paine.

> PAINE *fetches a lantern, pulls down a sheet, and turns out the light. While he is doing this,* CALLOWAY *cheerfully changes the subject.*

CALLOWAY : You know Paine's one of your devoted readers. He's promised to lend me — what is it? ' The Lone Rider '?

> MARTINS *does not reply.*

PAINE : I'd like to see Texas before I die, sir.

> MARTINS'S *nerves give way.*

MARTINS : Show me what you've got to show and let me get out.

> PAINE *works the slides. The first slide is of a man caught unawares by the camera —* HARBIN. *He is talking to some friends.*

[CALLOWAY : We put the screws on one of the racketeers' agents, an orderly in a military hospital. That's him. A chap called Harbin. He led us to Kurtz and Lime. Next, Paine.

> *The next slide is the photostat of a note which is signed by* HARRY LIME.

CALLOWAY : Can you identify that?

MARTINS : It's Harry's hand.

CALLOWAY : You see what I mean?

> *A world is beginning to come to an end for* MARTINS, *a world of easy friendship, hero-worship, confidence that had begun twenty years before . . . but he will not admit it. He sips his whisky . . .*

MARTINS : It *looks* like Harry's hand. But people are framed sometimes, Callaghan, even by the police. Why should Harry do a thing like that?

CALLOWAY : For seventy pounds a tube.][60]

MARTINS : I'd like a word with your agent, Harbin.

CALLOWAY : So would I.

---

[60] In the film, the following speech now appears:
CALLOWAY : See this man here? Fellow called Harbin, a medical orderly at the General Hospital. He worked for Lime and helped to steal the stuff from the laboratory. We forced him to give information, which led us as far as Kurtz and Lime, but we didn't arrest them as our evidence wasn't complete and it might have spoilt our chances of getting the others. Next.

MARTINS : Bring him in then.

CALLOWAY : I can't. He disappeared a week ago.

MARTINS : That's convenient. [A missing man witness against a dead man.]⁶¹

CALLOWAY : We have better witnesses.

Dissolve.

82. MONTAGE (NIGHT):

Microscope — finger prints, threads from coat, files about Lime — still photographs — and MARTINS'S *reaction to all this. Dissolve. (Still on page 52)*

83. CALLOWAY'S OFFICE (NIGHT):

CALLOWAY *is dropping a pile of photographs on his desk.* MARTINS *is sunk in a chair. He has nothing, at first, to say; he is convinced.*⁶²

CALLOWAY *kindly*: You see how it is, Martins. MARTINS *gets up and drinks his whisky.* Go back to bed, and keep out of trouble. You're all right in the hotel, and I'll try to fix things with the Austrian police, but I can't be responsible for you on the streets.

MARTINS : I'm not asking you to be.

CALLOWAY : I'm sorry, Martins.

MARTINS : [Awkward. Sorry. What a vocabulary you English have got.]⁶³

He goes. CALLOWAY *picks up the receiver.*

CALLOWAY : Get me the Austrian Police H.Q.

While he waits for the call to come through, BRODSKY *enters.*

BRODSKY : Can I have that passport? The Schmidt one?

It lies on CALLOWAY'S *desk. He pushes it with a ruler towards* BRODSKY.

CALLOWAY : We're not going to pick her up for that, are we?

BRODSKY : We treat these things more seriously, and your colleagues have agreed.

---

⁶¹ In the film, MARTINS adds: ' This is more like a mortuary than a Police H.Q. '

⁶² In the film, MARTINS then says: ' How could he have done it? '

⁶³ In the film, the dialogue is:

MARTINS : I'm sorry, too. *To* PAINE. Still got that aeroplane ticket on you?

CALLOWAY: We'll send it to the hotel in the morning.

Brodsky *exits with passport. Dissolve.*[64]

[84. SACHER'S HOTEL. RECEPTION DESK
(NIGHT):
Martins *goes up to the desk.*

Martins : 256, please.

Porter : I'm afraid your room has been cancelled, sir.

Martins : Cancelled?

Porter : We received instructions, sir, from Captain Carter.
They need the room.

Martins : What can I do?

Porter : Captain Carter suggested you could sleep in the
lounge for tonight. Martins *looks in the lounge full of officers
and their wives.* It will be quieter after one, sir. I'll find you a
blanket.

Martins : It's a drink I need.

85. SACHER'S BAR (NIGHT):
Carter *and* Tombs *stand at the bar, glasses in hand.*

Tombs: Don't look round, old chap. It's that fellow. We don't
want a scene.

Martins *pushes by to the bar, and pulls out a dollar
note.*

Barman : We aren't allowed to take those, sir.

Martins : Be a good fellow and change me one note.

Barman : I'm sorry, sir. It's against the rules.

Martins : But what can I do for money?

The Barman *whispers in his ear as he leads him to the
door. Dissolve.*

86. THE ORIENTAL. LOCATION (NIGHT):
*An International Police car drives up and the patrol
enters through a door marked: ' Out of Bounds to Allied
Personnel.'*

87. THE ORIENTAL : BAR AND DANCE FLOOR
(NIGHT):
The patrol enters. It is a dreary, smoky little night club.

---

[64] In the film, the following scene is substituted :
A CABARET BAR (NIGHT):
Martins *sits in a sleazy cabaret bar, drinking and watching the
floor show. Hostesses watch him, and a waiter brings him
another drink. An old flower-seller persuades him to buy two
huge bunches of chrysanthemums. Dissolve.*

The same semi-nude photographs on the stairs, the same half-drunk Americans at the bar, the same bad wine and extraordinary gins — you might be in any third-rate night haunt in any other shabby capital of a shabby Europe. A waiter is handing out a large pile of notes to MARTINS. *The cabaret is on and the International Patrol wait and take a look at the scene. The Americans at the bar never stir, and nobody interferes with them. The cabaret comes to an end.* MARTINS *rises. One of the dance girls, who has been watching the waiter give him the notes, comes up and speaks to him.*

DANCE GIRL : It's early, dear.

MARTINS : What? What did you say?

DANCE GIRL *puzzled* : It's early.

He looks at her as if he does not understand a word and goes to the stairs. Then he comes back to the GIRL *who is watching him.*

MARTINS : Did you ever know a fellow called Lime?

DANCE GIRL : No. Did you?

MARTINS shakes his head, less as if he were saying no than getting something out of his hair. Dissolve.

88. EMPTY CLUB (NIGHT) :
The seats are being piled up and a waiter and a girl are quietly pushing MARTINS *out.*

89. ANNA'S STREET (NIGHT) :
MARTINS *is walking unsteadily in the street. The rain is dripping from gutters, but he has not bothered to put on a coat.*

90. ANNA'S LANDING (NIGHT) :
MARTINS *knocks on the door and* ANNA *opens it. She is in a dressing-gown.*

ANNA : What is it? What's happened to you?

MARTINS : I've found out everything.

ANNA : Come in. You don't want to wake the house.]⁶⁵

---

⁶⁵ In the film, the scene begins in ANNA'S room as follows:
There is a knock at the door and ANNA *stirs.*
ANNA: Who's that?
MARTINS: It's me.
She opens the door. MARTINS *removes his hat, still holding the bunches of flowers. (Continued over.)*

91. ANNA'S ROOM (NIGHT):

ANNA: Now, what is it? I thought you were going to keep away. Are the police after you?

MARTINS: I don't know.

ANNA: You're drunk, aren't you?

MARTINS *sulkily*: A bit. *Angrily*. I'm sorry.[66]

[ANNA: Why? Wish I had a drink.

MARTINS: I've been with Calloway. Learnt everything. We were both wrong.

ANNA: You'd better tell me.

> *She sits down on the bed and he begins to tell her, swaying slightly with his back to the window.*

MARTINS: You know what penicillin does.

ANNA: Not really.

MARTINS: It's supposed to cure people of things. They've been stealing penicillin here, mixing it with water, I don't know what. People have been dying from it — wounded people, children. I suppose they were all in it — Kurtz, Tyler — even that doctor.]

ANNA: What is it? What happened to you?

MARTINS: Just came to see you.

[66] In the film, the scene continues:

MARTINS: I did want to say good bye before I pushed off back home.

ANNA: Why?

MARTINS: It's what you've always wanted, all of you. *Dangles a string to the cat on the bed*. Kitty. *The cat jumps off the bed*. Not very sociable, is he?

ANNA: No, he only likes cats. What made you decide so suddenly?

MARTINS: I brought you these . . . *Offers flowers*. They got a little wet, but . . .

ANNA: What happened to your hand?

MARTINS: A parrot . . .

ANNA: Have you seen Calloway?

MARTINS: Imagine a parrot nipping a man.

ANNA: Have you?

MARTINS: Oh . . . I've been saying good bye all over.

ANNA: He told you, didn't he?

MARTINS: Told me?

ANNA: About Harry.

MARTINS: You know?

ANNA: I've seen Major Calloway today.

> *Camera tracks to the window and shows the square outside.*

82

He goes to the window, and turns again to her. Over his shoulder we look down into the dark street.

92. ANNA'S STREET. LOCATION (NIGHT):
Somebody looks up at the lighted window. The shadow of a bombed building falls across his face so that we cannot see it. He walks towards a door and stands in the shadow — we cannot see him — a cat walks across from the other side of the road in his direction — it is mewing.

93. DOORWAY. LOCATION (NIGHT):
The cat comes to the man's legs — purring and rubs itself around the bottom of his trouser-leg — it is hungry.

94. ANNA'S ROOM (NIGHT):
[MARTINS: I'm not a doctor: I don't understand it all, except Harry made seventy pounds a tube — he ran the business.

> ANNA *looks away from the laughing, cheery photograph of* HARRY.

ANNA: You were sober when they told you? They really proved it?

MARTINS: Yes. So you see, that was Harry.

> ANNA *puts her hand over her eyes.*]

ANNA: He's better dead. I thought perhaps he was mixed up . . . but not with that.

MARTINS *getting up and walking about*: For twenty years — I knew him — the drinks he liked, the girls he liked. We laughed at the same things. He couldn't bear the colour green. But it wasn't true. He never existed, we dreamed him. Was he laughing at fools like us all the time?

ANNA *sadly*: He liked to laugh.

MARTINS *bitterly*: Seventy pounds a tube. And he asked me to write about his great medical charity. I suppose he wanted a Press Agent. Maybe I could have raised the price to eighty pounds.

ANNA: There are so many things you don't know about a person you love, good things, bad things.

MARTINS: But to cash in like that . . .

ANNA *angrily*: For heaven's sake, stop making him in *your* image. Harry was real. He wasn't just your friend and my lover. He was Harry.

MARTINS : Don't talk wisdom at me. You make it sound as if his manners were occasionally bad . . . I don't know . . . I'm just a bad writer who drinks too much and falls in love with girls . . . [lots of girls] . . . you.

ANNA : Me?

MARTINS : Don't be such a fool — you know I love you?

ANNA : If you'd rung me up and asked me, were you dark or fair or had a moustache, I wouldn't have known.

MARTINS : Can't you get him out of your head?

ANNA : No.

MARTINS : I'm leaving Vienna. I don't care if Kurtz killed Harry or Tyler — or the third man. Whoever killed him, it was justice. Maybe I'd have killed him myself.

ANNA : A man doesn't alter because you find out more.

MARTINS : I hate the way you talk. I've got a splitting headache, and you talk and talk . . . You make me cross.

Suddenly ANNA *laughs.*

ANNA : You come here at three in the morning — a stranger — and say you love me. Then you get angry and pick a quarrel. What do you expect me to do?

MARTINS : I haven't seen you laugh before. Do it again. I like it.

ANNA *staring through him* : There isn't enough for two laughs.

> MARTINS *takes her by the shoulder and shakes her gently.*

MARTINS : I'd make comic faces all day long. I'd stand on my head and grin at you between my legs. I'd learn a lot of jokes from the books on After Dinner Speaking . . . I'd . . .

> ANNA *stares at him without speaking.*

MARTINS *hopelessly* : You still love Harry, don't you?

[ANNA *picking up the copy of her play* : I've got to learn my lines.

> ANNA *looks through the pages of her script and back to* MARTINS. MARTINS *drops his hands. As he goes towards the door, he turns and makes half an apology, half an accusation.*]

Martins : You told me to find a girl.

Dissolve.

95. ANNA'S STREET. LOCATION (NIGHT) :

Martins *walks rapidly away. Passing along the street,
he becomes aware of a figure in a doorway on the
opposite side of the street. The whole figure is in darkness except for the points of the shoes.* Martins *stops and
stares and the silent motionless figure in the dark street
stares back at him.* Martins's *nerves are on edge. Is this
one of* Calloway's *men, or* Tyler's, *or the Austrian
police?*

[Martins *sharply* : Do you want anything?

No reply. Martins *takes a few steps on and then turns
again.*]

Martins : Have you been following me? Who's your boss?

Still no reply. Martins *is irascible with drink. He calls out
sharply.* Can't you answer?[67]

*A window curtain opposite is drawn back and a sleepy
voice shouts angrily to him.*

Woman : Seien Sie ruhig. Gehen Sie weiter. (Be quiet. Go
away.)

The light shines across straight on the other man's face.

Martins : Harry!

Martins, *in his amazement, hesitates on the edge of the
pavement. The woman has slammed down the window
and the figure is again in darkness, except for the shoe-
caps. Then it begins to emerge, but before* Martins *has
a chance of seeing the face again, an International
Police car approaches down the street. The figure steps
back, and as the car comes between them, the figure
makes off in the dark. By the time the car has passed, there is no sign
of the stranger — only the sound of footsteps.* Martins *pursues,
but the sound dies out. He passes a kiosk and comes out into a fairly
well-lighted square which is completely empty. He stands around in*

---

[67] In the film, Martins begins his speech with the line : ' What kind
of a spy do you think you are, satchel-foot? ' and ends it with the
line. chanting childishly : ' Come out, come out, whoever you are.'

bewilderment, unable to decide whether he was drunk or whether he had seen a ghost, or indeed HARRY. *Dissolve.*

96. KIOSK SQUARE. LOCATION (NIGHT):
CALLOWAY *stands looking at the square with* MARTINS *and* PAINE.

MARTINS : You don't believe me ...

CALLOWAY : No.

MARTINS : It ran up here and vanished.
They stare at the empty moonlit square. PAINE *and* CALLOWAY *exchange glances.*

CALLOWAY : Where were you when you saw it first?

MARTINS : Down there — fifty yards away.
CALLOWAY *turns his back on the square and looks down the street past the kiosk.*

CALLOWAY : Which side of the road?

MARTINS : This one. And there aren't any side turnings.
They begin to walk down the street.

CALLOWAY : Doorways ...

MARTINS : But I could hear it running ahead of me.
They reach the kiosk.

CALLOWAY : And it vanished with a puff of smoke, I suppose, and a clap of ... *He breaks off as his eye lights on the kiosk, and he walks across to it, pulls open the door. We see the little curling staircase going down.* It wasn't the German gin, Paine.
CALLOWAY *leads the way down, shining a torch ahead.*

97. THE SEWERS. LOCATION (NIGHT):
A strange world unknown to most of us lies under our feet: a cavernous land of waterfalls and rushing rivers, where tides ebb and flow as in the world above. The main sewer, half as wide as the Thames, rushes by under a huge arch, fed by tributary streams: these streams have fallen in waterfalls from higher levels and have been purified in their falls, so that only in these side channels is the air foul. The main stream smells sweet and fresh with a faint tang of ozone, and everywhere in the darkness is the sound of falling and rushing water.

MARTINS : What is it?

CALLOWAY *without replying moves ahead, across a bridge which spans a waterfall.*

PAINE: It's only the main sewer, sir. Smells sweet, don't it? [They used it as an air-raid shelter in the war, just like our old tube.][68]

They come up with CALLOWAY *who is leaning over the bridge.*

CALLOWAY: I've been a fool. We should have dug deeper than a grave. *Dissolve.*

98. CENTRAL CEMETERY. LOCATION (DAWN):

[*A small group make their way down an avenue of graves. At the end of the avenue three men are engaged in digging. The group consists of* CALLOWAY, *a* BRITISH JUNIOR OFFICER, MARTINS, *an Austrian* POLICE OFFICER, *and an* OFFICIAL *from the City Council, who carries an umbrella. The group pass the graves of Beethoven, Schubert, and Brahms, and* CALLOWAY *pauses just long enough for us to take in their inscriptions. As they approach* LIME'S *grave, thin rain begins to fall, and the Austrian* OFFICIAL *opens his umbrella and offers to share it with* CALLOWAY.] *One of the men comes over to* CALLOWAY *and speaks in German.*

MAN: Wir sind jetzt am Sarg. (We've reached the coffin.)

CALLOWAY *to* OFFICIAL: Tell them to take off the lid.

CALLOWAY *and the* OFFICIAL, *still under the same umbrella, go up to the graveside and stand looking down. The* OFFICIAL *moves round the side of the grave to examine the body from another angle. He turns across the grave to* CALLOWAY *and shrugs his shoulders.* CALLOWAY *takes one look and moves away, passing* MARTINS. *He nods to* MARTINS *to take a look.* MARTINS *reluctantly does so, then quietly joins* CALLOWAY *as they walk away.*

OFFICIAL: Did you know him, Colonel?

CALLOWAY: Yes. Joseph Harbin, medical orderly at the 43rd General Hospital. *To* JUNIOR OFFICER. Next time we'll have a fool-proof coffin. *Dissolve.*

---

[68] In the film, PAINE adds: ' Runs right into the blue Danube.'

99. INTERNATIONAL POLICE H.Q. (DAWN):
A doorway marked International Police in three languages. Through the door comes BRODSKY with ANNA's passport. He crosses over the hallway and out into the yard where the International Police car is waiting. He goes up to the car and the RUSSIAN member of the patrol gets out and joins him. He speaks to him. Dissolve.

100. ANNA'S STREET. LOCATION (DAWN):
The International Police Patrol drives up and, leaving an Austrian policeman in the car, enters the building.

101. STAIRCASE AND LANDING (DAWN):
The four men run up the stairs, the BRITISH M.P. leading. At ANNA's door, the BRITISH M.P. tries the handle. The RUSSIAN M.P. pushing forward, puts his shoulder to it and breaks in. ANNA has not had time to get out of bed.

102. ANNA'S ROOM (DAWN):
ANNA: Was ist es? (What is it?)

RUSSIAN M.P.: Sie müssen mit uns kommen. (You must come with us.)[69]

ANNA *to the* BRITISH *and* AMERICAN M.P's: Have I got to go?

BRITISH M.P.: Sorry, miss, it's orders.

RUSSIAN M.P. *in bad German*: These your papers? Your papers?

He shows ANNA's *passport.* ANNA *looks at them and up to the four men, realising there is nothing she can do.*[70]

[ANNA: Please tell him to go while I dress.

AMERICAN M.P. *to* RUSSIAN M.P. *in very bad German*: Komm in die Vorraum bis sie angezogen. (Come in the passage while she gets her things on.)

RUSSIAN M.P.: Nein, nein.

BRITISH M.P.: I'm not staying here. Let the girl dress by herself. *He prepares to leave.*

AMERICAN M.P.: You can't leave a little goil alone with Rusky here. I'd better stay.

---

[69] In the film, the Russian M.P. begins: 'Internationale Polizei.'
[70] In the film, ANNA merely leaves the room to dress.

British M.P. *to* French M.P.: You coming, Froggy? *The* French M.P. *is amused and speaks in French.*

French M.P.: Qu'est-ce-ça fait? (What does it matter?) I will look after both of them.

> *The* British M.P. *goes out of the room. The* American M.P. *stays in the room and keeps his back chivalrously turned, but he is restless and takes a bit of chewing-gum. The* French M.P. *thinks it fun, lights a cigarette and watches with detached, amused interest the attitude of the other two. The* Russian M.P. *is just doing his duty and watches the girl closely all the time without sexual interest.*]

103. ANNA'S LANDING (DAWN):

> *The* British M.P. *stands by the wall, yawning. The* Woman *who owns the house comes up and speaks to him in German.*

Woman *in German*: This happens every day. I am getting tired of the police.

> *He does not understand a word and to escape from her goes back into the room.*

104. ANNA'S ROOM (DAWN):

> Anna *has finished dressing as the* British M.P. *enters.*

Anna: Where are you taking me?

American M.P.: International Police Headquarters for a check-up. The Russkies are claiming the body.

Anna: Body?

American M.P.: Just an expression.

> *The* Russian M.P. *listens suspiciously to their conversation.*

British M.P.: It's the law, miss. We can't go against the protocol.

Anna: I don't even know what protocol means.

British M.P.: I don't either, miss.

Russian M.P.: Wir müssen gehen. (We must go.)

> Anna *picks up her bag. The* Russian M.P. *takes it away from her and looks rapidly through the contents, and then hands it back.*

[French M.P.: Mademoiselle, your lipstick.

> *He picks her lipstick from the dressing-table and hands*

it to her. The BRITISH *and* AMERICAN *M.P's go ahead
out of the room. The* RUSSIAN *next, then* ANNA, *then the*
FRENCH *M.P. tall and undisturbed and uninterested
with his dangling cigarette. In the doorway* ANNA *suddenly turns and says hopelessly to the divan, the table,
the walls . . .*

ANNA : Good bye.

The RUSSIAN *swings round with his gun pointing, but
there is no one in the room. The* FRENCH *M.P. laughs.
Dissolve.*]

105. HALL. INTERNATIONAL POLICE H.Q. (DAWN):
MARTINS *is by the stairs when the International Patrol
brings* ANNA *in.*

MARTINS *with astonishment* : Anna.

AMERICAN M.P. : You can't talk to the prisoner, son.

MARTINS : Why are you here? ANNA *shrugs her shoulders.*
I've got to talk to you. I've just seen a dead man walking.

ANNA *looks up sharply. They begin to move up the
stairs and* MARTINS *follows.*

MARTINS : I saw him buried, and now I've seen him alive.

AMERICAN M.P. : Please, Jock . . . I don't want no trouble
with you . . .

ANNA *looks at* MARTINS *with excitement, She cannot
bring herself to believe him.*

ANNA : You're drunk?

MARTINS : No.

They come to the head of the stairs. CALLOWAY *is about
to enter his office — he sees the group who are about to
pass on.*

CALLOWAY : One moment . . . Bring the prisoner in here.
He motions to the patrol to wait outside. The BRITISH
M.P. *jerks his hand for* ANNA *to enter and* MARTINS
tries to follow.

AMERICAN M.P. : Not you.

He pushes him away and the door is slammed on him.

106. CALLOWAY'S OFFICE (DAY):
ANNA *is brought in.* PAINE *is in the office.*

CALLOWAY : Sit down, Miss Schmidt. The Russians have
asked for you, but I'm not interested in your forged papers.

She sits down. She is strung up with excitement at what she has heard from MARTINS. *She is waiting to have her hopes confirmed or darkened.*

CALLOWAY : When did you last see Lime?

ANNA : Two weeks ago. *She waits hungrily for his next question.*

CALLOWAY : We want the truth, Miss Schmidt . . . We know he's alive.

ANNA *with excitement and joy* : It *is* true, then?

CALLOWAY : The body of another man, Joseph Harbin, was found in the coffin.

   ANNA *cannot attend to anything but this news.*

ANNA : What did you say? I didn't hear you. I'm sorry.

CALLOWAY : I said another man was buried in his place.

ANNA : Another man? Oh, yes . . . where's Harry?

CALLOWAY : That's what we want to find out.

ANNA : I'm sorry. I don't seem able to understand anything you say. But nothing matters now. He's [safe.][71]

[CALLOWAY : I wouldn't say safe.

ANNA : He's alive. Now, this minute he's doing something. He's breathing.]

CALLOWAY : We are pretty sure, Miss Schmidt, that he's somewhere in the Russian sector, across the canal. Sooner or later we'll get him, even if the Russians don't co-operate. You may as well help us.

ANNA : Help you? Why?

CALLOWAY : The next man you have to deal with is Colonel Brodsky. Tell me where Lime is?

ANNA : I don't know . . .

CALLOWAY : If you help us, we are prepared to help you.

ANNA : Martins always said you were a fool.

CALLOWAY : Miss Schmidt, Vienna is a closed city. A rat would have more chance in a closed room without a hole and a pack of terriers loose.

ANNA : Poor Harry. *All her joy has gone now.* I wish he *was* dead. He'd be safe from all of you then.

CALLOWAY : Better think about it. *He goes to the door and*

---

[71] In the film, ANNA says : '. . . alive.'

out.[72]

[107. HALL. INTERNATIONAL POLICE H.Q. (DAY):
MARTINS *waits at the bottom of the staircase.* CALLOWAY
comes slowly down.

MARTINS : What are you doing with her?

CALLOWAY : Her? *He is lost in thought.* Paine! PAINE *comes
out from the side room.*

PAINE : Sir?

MARTINS : Anna, of course. What's going on?

CALLOWAY : The Russians claim the body, Martins.

MARTINS : You aren't going to hand her over?

CALLOWAY : Her papers are false.

MARTINS : Why, you double-timing . . .

CALLOWAY : She's no concern of mine, Martins. It's Lime I
want.

MARTINS : Damn Lime.

CALLOWAY *continues through the door with* PAINE.
Dissolve.

108. CASANOVA (DAY):
MARTINS *enters and goes to the* HEAD WAITER *after
vainly looking for* KURTZ *upon the floor, where a tea-
dance is in progress.*

MARTINS : Is Baron von Kurtz here?

HEAD WAITER : I do not know the Baron.

MARTINS : Oh, yes, you do. He plays in your orchestra.

HEAD WAITER : The Baron von . . .?

MARTINS : Kurtz. Kurtz.

HEAD WAITER : We have someone called Freddie Kurtz, but
he hasn't turned up today.

MARTINS : With a *toupée.*

HEAD WAITER : That is right. His mother works in the
cloakroom.

As MARTINS *goes up the stairs to the cloakroom, the
door of the club opens and the International Patrol
enters, accompanied by Austrian police. The Austrians
stand guard at the door, two* M.P*'s go down to the dance*

---

[72] In the film, there is a dissolve straight to the adapted beginning of
the sequence in front of KURTZ's house. [See note 73]

floor and do a check of papers there. The others remain above.

109. CLOAKROOM (DAY):

A slatternly woman with a malevolent sour face is looking after the cloakroom.

AMERICAN M.P.: Papers, please.

She hands him her papers. MARTINS *stands by watching.*

AMERICAN M.P.: Frau Kurtz?

FRAU KURTZ: Ja.

She blows her nose with her fingers. Reaction on MARTINS, *who has expected to see an aristocratic woman turning her head nobly to plebeian tasks.*

BRITISH M.P. *to* MARTINS: Passport, please sir. *He looks through it, and hands it back.* Where are you staying?

MARTINS: Nowhere. I've been turned out of the only room I had.

BRITISH M.P.: If you'll call at the station, we'll do what we can for you, sir.

MARTINS: You'll find me a bed, will you, but you can't find Harry Lime.

The M.P. *gives him a quick look and hands back the passport.*

AMERICAN M.P.: Give us time.

The other M.P's *have rejoined them and they go out together.* MARTINS *turns to* FRAU KURTZ.

MARTINS: You really are Frau Kurtz?

FRAU KURTZ: Ja.

MARTINS: Sprechen Sie Englisch?

FRAU KURTZ: Little. Very little.

MARTINS: I know your son. I thought I'd find him here.

FRAU KURTZ: Freddie?

MARTINS: The Baron.

FRAU KURTZ goes off into a peal of laughter, showing one long dirty tooth like a fossil.

FRAU KURTZ: Baron? His father was a butcher in Linz. He will be at home today. It is safer so, nein?

Dissolve.

110. BRIDGE. LOCATION (DAY):

MARTINS *walks up from the makeshift bridge over the*

93

*canal, past the sign that warns one is entering the Russian
zone, and into the long wide dingy Praterstrasse. In a
side-turning are a number of big houses that have come
down in the world through bombing and abandonment.
He consults his notebook for* KURTZ'S *address.* MARTINS
*stops outside one house. The bottom floor is gutted, and
the doorway smashed in, but the first floor is habitable.
A balcony, half-broken away, is in front of the windows.*
MARTINS *bangs on the smashed door with his fist, then
finds a makeshift wire bell and pulls it. It jangles somewhere above, and* MARTINS *steps back into the roadway
and waits. One of the windows opens and* KURTZ *looks
out. When he sees* MARTINS, *he comes forward cautiously
onto the smashed balcony.]*[73]

KURTZ : [Why, Rollo, you?] Winkel, look who's here.

WINKEL *comes out and joins him on the balcony.*

MARTINS : I want to speak to you, Kurtz.

KURTZ : Of course. [Come in.]

MARTINS : [I'd rather stay where I am. You might be following your father's profession.][74]

KURTZ : I don't understand . . .

MARTINS : [I've been talking to your mother. Now] I want to
talk to Harry, Kurtz.

KURTZ : Are you mad?

MARTINS : [Never mind that. Say I'm mad, say] I've seen a
ghost. But you tell Harry I want to see him.

> [*He looks around and sees, between the gap in the
> shelled houses, the Great Wheel in the fairground.*]

KURTZ : Be reasonable. Come up and talk.

MARTINS : I like the open. [I like crowds.] Tell him I'll wait
by the Wheel for an hour. Or do ghosts only rise by night?
Have you an opinion on that, Dr. Winkel?

---

[73] In the film, the scene begins as follows:

THE STREET OUTSIDE KURTZ'S HOUSE (DAY):

> MARTINS *comes across the courtyard to the house and rings the
> doorbell.* KURTZ *comes onto the balcony in his dressing-gown.*

KURTZ: Why, that's you! Come up! . . .

[74] In the film, the dialogue runs:

KURTZ : . . . Come up.

MARTINS : I'll wait here.

DR. WINKEL *takes out his handkerchief and blows his nose.* MARTINS *walks away towards the Great Wheel. Dissolve.*

111. THE GREAT WHEEL. PART LOCATION (DAY):
The Wheel on this cold autumn day is not popular, and the Prater itself has not recovered sufficiently from the shelling and bombing to attract crowds. A wrecked pleasure place, weeds growing up round the foundations of merry-go-rounds. In the enclosure one stall is selling big thin flat cakes like cart-wheels, and the children queue with coupons. A few courting couples wait and wait on the platform of the wheel, and then are packed into a single car and revolve slowly above the city with empty cars above and below them. As the loaded car reaches the highest point of the Wheel, the machinery stops for a couple of minutes and leaves them suspended. Looking up, MARTINS can see the tiny faces pressed like flies against a glass. He walks up and down to keep warm. He looks at his watch. The time is nearly up. (Still on cover) Somewhere behind the cake stall, someone is whistling. MARTINS turns quickly. He watches for him to come into sight with fear and excitement. Life to MARTINS has always quickened when HARRY came, as he comes now, as though nothing much has really happened: with an amused geniality, a recognition that his happiness will make the world's day. Only sometimes the cheerfulness will be suddenly clouded; a melancholy beats through his guard; a memory that this life does not go on. Now he does not make the mistake of offering a hand that might be rejected, but instead just pats MARTINS on his bandaged hand.

HARRY: How are things? They seem to have been messing you about a bit.

MARTINS: We've got to talk, Harry.

HARRY: Of course, old man. This way.
He walks straight on towards the platform in the absolute confidence that MARTINS *will follow.*

MARTINS: Alone.
The Wheel has come round again and one lot of passen-

gers is getting out on the opposite platform as another enters the same car from their platform. HARRY has always known the ropes everywhere, so now he speaks apart to the PORTRESS and money passes. The car with the passengers moves slowily up, an empty car passes, and then the Wheel stops long enough for them to get into the third car, which they have to themselves.

112. GREAT WHEEL: BACK PROJECTION (DAY):

HARRY : We couldn't be more alone. Lovers used to do this in the old days, but they haven't the money to spare, poor devils, now.

113. TOP SHOT FROM GREAT WHEEL (DAY):

He looks out of the window of the swaying, rising car at the figures diminishing below them with what looks like genuine commiseration. Very slowly, on one side of them, the city sinks: very slowly on the other, the great cross girders of the Wheel rise into sight. As the horizon slides away, the Danube becomes visible, and the piers of the Reichsbrucke lift above the houses.

114. GREAT WHEEL: BACK PROJECTION (DAY):

HARRY turns from the window.

HARRY : It's good to see you, Rollo.

MARTINS : I was at your funeral.

HARRY : That was pretty smart, wasn't it?

MARTINS : You know what's happened to Anna? They've arrested her.

HARRY : Tough, very tough, but don't worry, old man. They won't hurt her.

MARTINS : They are handing her to the Russians. Can't you help her?

HARRY *unconvincingly* : What can I do, old man? I'm dead — aren't I? Who have you told about me?

MARTINS : The police — and Anna.

HARRY : Unwise, Rollo, unwise. Did they believe you?

MARTINS : You don't care a damn about her, do you?

HARRY : I've got a lot on my mind.

MARTINS: You won't do a thing to help her?

HARRY : What can I do, Rollo? Be reasonable. Give myself up? This is a far far better thing. The old limelight and the fall of the curtain. We aren't heroes, Rollo, you and I. The world doesn't make heroes outside your books.

MARTINS : You have your contacts.

HARRY : I've got to be so careful. These Russians, Rollo — well, I'm safe so long as I have my uses.

MARTINS *with sudden realisation* : You informed on her.

HARRY *with a smile* : Don't become a policeman, old man.

MARTINS : I didn't believe the police when they told me about you. Were you going to cut me in on the spoils?

HARRY : I've never kept you out of anything, old man, yet.

> HARRY *stands with his back to the door as the car swings upward and smiles back at* MARTINS.

MARTINS : I remember that time at that Club ' The 43 ',when the police raided it. You'd learnt a safe way out. Absolutely safe for you. It wasn't safe for me.

HARRY : [You always were a clumsy devil, Rollo.][75]

MARTINS : You've never grown up, Harry.

HARRY : Well, we shall be old for a very long time.

MARTINS : Have you ever seen any of your victims?

> HARRY *takes a look at the toy landscape below and comes away from the door.*

HARRY : I never feel quite safe in these things. *He feels the door with his hands.* Victims? Don't be melodramatic. Look down there.

115. TOP SHOT FROM GREAT WHEEL :
LOCATION (DAY) :

> *He points through the window at the people moving like black flies at the base of the Wheel.*

116. GREAT WHEEL : BACK PROJECTION (DAY) :

HARRY : Would you really feel any pity if one of those dots stopped moving for ever? If I said you can have twenty thousand pounds for every dot that stops, would you really, old man, tell me to keep my money — or would you calculate how many dots you could afford to spare? Free of income tax, old man. Free of income tax. *He gives his boyish, conspiratorial smile.* It's the only way to save nowadays.

MARTINS : You're finished now. The police know everything.

---

75 In the film, HARRY says : ' You should never have gone to the police, you know. You should have left this thing alone.'

HARRY : But they can't catch me, Rollo. They can't come in the Russian Zone.

[*The car swings to a standstill at the highest point of the curve and* HARRY *turns his back and gazes out of the window.* MARTINS *draws his arms back: he thinks one good shove would be strong enough to break the glass. His arms drop again.*

MARTINS : The police have dug up your coffin.

HARRY : I couldn't trust Harbin. Look at the sunset, Rollo.

MARTINS *looking at the sunset* : You know I love Anna.

HARRY : That's fine, old man. If she gets out of this hole, be kind to her. She's worth it.

He gives the impression of having arranged everything to everybody's satisfaction.

MARTINS : I'd like to knock you through the window.

HARRY : But you won't, old man. Our quarrels never lasted long. You remember that time in the Monaco, Kurtz tried to persuade me to, well, arrange an accident.

MARTINS : It wouldn't be easy.

HARRY : I carry a gun. You don't think they'd look for a bullet wound after you hit *that* ground.][76]

Again the car begins to move, sailing slowly down, until the flies are midgets, are recognisable human beings.

HARRY : What fools we are, Rollo, talking like this, as if I'd do that to you — or you to me. *Deliberately he turns his back and leans his face against the glass.* In these days, old man, nobody thinks in terms of human beings. Governments don't, so why should we? They talk of the people and the proletariat, and I talk of the mugs. It's the same thing. They have their five year plans and so have I. *(Still on page 53)*

MARTINS : You used to believe in a God.

---

[76] In the film, the dialogue of this sequence is:

MARTINS *looking out of the window* : I should be pretty easy to get rid of.

HARRY : Pretty easy.

MARTINS : Don't be too sure.

HARRY : I carry a gun. You don't think they'd look for a bullet wound after you hit *that* ground.

MARTINS : They dug up your coffin.

HARRY : Found Harbin? Pity.

That shade of melancholy crosses HARRY'S *face.*

HARRY: Oh, I still *believe*, old man. In God and Mercy and all that. The dead are happier dead. They don't miss much here, poor devils.

> *As he speaks the last words with the odd touch of genuine pity, the car reaches the platform and the faces of the doomed-to-be-victims peer in at them.*[77]

HARRY: I'd like to cut you in, you know. We always did things together, Rollo. I've no one left in Vienna I can really trust.

[MARTINS: Tyler? Winkel, Kurtz?

HARRY: The police are on to all of them now.

117. GREAT WHEEL: LOCATION (DAY):

> *They pass out of the car and* HARRY *puts his hand again on* MARTINS'S *elbow.*

HARRY: Have you heard anything of old Bracer recently?

MARTINS: I had a card at Christmas.

HARRY: Those were the days, old man. Those were the days.

MARTINS: You'd really cut me in, would you?

HARRY: There's plenty for two — with the others gone. Think it over, old man. Send me a message through Kurtz. I'll meet you anywhere, any time.

> *He has written the number on the back of an envelope.*
> MARTINS *holds it in his hand.*

HARRY: So long, Rollo.

> *He turns to go, and* MARTINS *calls after him.*

MARTINS: And Anna — you won't do a thing to help?

HARRY: If I could, old man, of course. But my hands are tied. *When he is a little further away, he suddenly comes back.* If we meet again, Rollo, it's you I want to see, and not the police. Remember, won't you?

> MARTINS *stands there watching the figure disappear.*

---

[77] In the film, there is more dialogue here:
MARTINS: What do you believe in?
HARRY: If you ever get Anna out of this mess, be kind to her. You'll find she's worth it. I wish I'd asked you to bring some of those tablets.
They get off the Wheel.

Dissolve.][78]

118. CALLOWAY'S OFFICE (DAY):

CALLOWAY *is standing with his back to* MARTINS *studying a map of Vienna.*

CALLOWAY: [We'd choose the right spot.][79]

MARTINS: It wouldn't work.

CALLOWAY: We'll never get him in the Russian Zone.

MARTINS: You expect too much, Callaghan. Oh, I know he deserves to hang. You've proved your stuff. But twenty [five] years is a long time. Don't ask me to tie the rope.[80]

MARTINS *moves up and down as he speaks. The door opens and Colonel* BRODSKY *enters.*

CALLOWAY: Evening, Brodsky. Anything I can do?

BRODSKY: We've identified the girl.

CALLOWAY: I've questioned her. We've got nothing against her.

BRODSKY: We shall apply for her at the Four Power meeting tomorrow.[81]

During their talk we watch MARTINS'S *reactions.*

CALLOWAY: I've asked your people to help with Lime.

BRODSKY: This is a different case. It is being looked into.

As he goes he drops ANNA'S *passport on* CALLOWAY'S *desk and smiles.*

[BRODSKY: It is very clever, but I thought I could rely on

---

[78] In the film, HARRY adds a famous parting speech:
'When you make up your mind, send me a message — I'll meet you any place, any time, and when we do meet, old man, it's you I want to see, not the police . . . and don't be so gloomy . . . After all, it's not that awful — you know what the fellow said . . . In Italy for thirty years under the Borgias they had warfare, terror, murder, bloodshed — they produced Michaelangelo, Leonardo da Vinci and the Renaissance. In Switzerland they had brotherly love, five hundred years of democracy and peace, and what did that produce . . .? The cuckoo clock. So long, Holly.'

[79] In the film, CALLOWAY says: 'Look here, Martins, you can always arrange to meet him in some little café . . . Say here,' . . . Pointing at the map . . . 'in the International Zone.'

[80] In the film, CALLOWAY answers' 'Okay, forget it.'

[81] In the film, BRODSKY adds a remark to each of his two speeches. The first is: 'This is her report', and he hands it to CALLOWAY. The second is: 'She has no right to be here.'

my information. Good night, colonel.

CALLOWAY : Good night.

> CALLOWAY *looks down at an open file which has a photograph of* LIME *in it.*]

CALLOWAY : In the last war a general would hang his opponent's picture on the wall. He got to know him that way. I'm beginning to know Lime, and I think this would have worked. With your help.

MARTINS : What price would you pay?

CALLOWAY : Name it.

> *Dissolve.*

119. VIENNA RAILWAY STATION BUFFET : BACK PROJECTION (NIGHT):

> *A clock shows 8.15 p.m. Atmosphere and description must be left for location.* [MARTINS *is standing, glass in hand, in the crowded buffet. The windows are frosted up, but whenever the door opens, the clang and clatter of the station and the steam of the engines blow in.* ANNA *and* PAINE *enter.* MARTINS *sees them, puts down his glass and begins to worm his way out. He does not want to be seen.*

PAINE : Well, miss, you'll be having breakfast in the British Zone. You needn't fear the Russkies with those papers.

ANNA : I don't understand a thing.

PAINE : If I picked up a pound note, miss, I'd put it quick in my pocket, no questions asked. I'll be saying good night.

ANNA : Good night. Thank you. How kind you've been.

> PAINE *goes out.* ANNA *looks at the ticket and papers he has given her, and then across the buffet. She sees* MARTINS *making for another door. Suspicions of what she does not yet know come to her.* MARTINS *looks back and meets her gaze — uneasily. He stops. Slowly she thrusts her way through the crowd at the buffet to his side.*

ANNA : What are you doing here?][82]

---

[82] In the film, the following sequence is substituted :

> MARTINS *begins by standing at the station barrier. He moves to the buffet to avoid* ANNA *and* PAINE, *who sees her onto the train, and finds a compartment for her. (Continued over.)*

MARTINS : I wanted to see you safely off. *Defiantly.* There's no harm in that, is there?

ANNA : How did you know I'd be here?

MARTINS sees he has made a mistake and becomes evasive.

MARTINS : Oh, I heard something about it at Police H.Q.

ANNA : Have you been seeing Colonel Calloway?

MARTINS : No. I don't live in his pocket.

ANNA : Harry, what is it?

MARTINS : For heaven's sake, don't call me Harry again.

ANNA : I'm sorry.

LOUDSPEAKER : Passengers for Klagenfurt take their seats, please.

The loudspeaker repeats it in French, German and Russian, while the dialogue goes on.

MARTINS : It's time to be off, Anna.

ANNA : What's on your mind, Rollo? Why did you avoid me just now?

MARTINS : I didn't see you. Anna, you *must* come along.

He urges her through the buffet door.

120. RAILWAY PLATFORM. BACK PROJECTION (NIGHT):

Reluctantly, scenting a mystery, ANNA follows MARTINS towards the train.

MARTINS : Only six hours. It's going to be cold. Take my coat.

ANNA : I shall be all right.

MARTINS begins to take off his coat.

PAINE : Here we are, you'll be all right here, miss.

ANNA : I'm afraid I don't understand Major Calloway.

PAINE : I expect he's got a soft spot for you, miss.

ANNA : Why has he done it?

PAINE : Don't you worry, miss, you're well out of things. There we are, miss.

ANNA : Thank you, you've been so kind.

PAINE : Well, I'll be saying good night.

PAINE leaves, while ANNA inspects her ticket and papers. She looks out of the train window, sees MARTINS in the buffet, and gets off the train to accost him there. Then she asks: 'Are you going too?'

102

MARTINS : Send me a wire from Klagenfurt when you are safe.

ANNA : Are you staying in Vienna?

MARTINS *evasively*: A day or two. *He puts his coat round* ANNA *and opens a compartment door.* Jump in, my dear.

ANNA : What's going to happen? Where is he?

MARTINS : Safe in the Russian Zone. I saw him today.

ANNA : You saw him?

MARTINS : Oh yes, we talked and he laughed a lot. Like the old days.

ANNA : How is he?

MARTINS : He can look after himself. Don't worry.

ANNA : Did he say anything about me?

MARTINS : Oh, the usual things.

ANNA : What?

[MARTINS : He's untouchable, Anna. Why, he even wanted to cut me in.

> *Doors of compartments are being slammed. A porter approaches.*

PORTER : Please get in.]

MARTINS : Goodbye, Anna.

ANNA : I don't want to go.

MARTINS : You must.

ANNA : There's something wrong. Did you tell Calloway about your meeting?

MARTINS : No. Of course, not.

ANNA : Why should Calloway be helping me like this? The Russians will make trouble.

MARTINS : That's his headache.

> [*A* SOLDIER *comes up to him.*

SOLDIER : Colonel Calloway's compliments, sir, and the car's waiting. We've got to get started.

ANNA : Why did you lie? . . . What are you two doing?]

MARTINS : We're getting you out of here.

ANNA : I'm not going.

MARTINS : You must. *He puts his hand on her arm as though to force her into the carriage.* [You are more important than a crook like that. Get in.

> *She shakes herself free.*

107

ANNA : What are you doing?

MARTINS *angrily, his nerves breaking*: They want my help and I'm giving it them.

ANNA : The police?

MARTINS : For pete's sake get in.

ANNA : And you have the nerve to talk about love. Love for me, love for Harry. How do you spell the word?

MARTINS : I asked him to help you, and he wouldn't lift a finger. He called you a good little thing, and said the Russians wouldn't hurt you.

ANNA : Poor Harry.

MARTINS : Why in heaven's name, poor Harry?][83]

ANNA : Oh, you've got your precious honesty, and don't want anything else.

MARTINS *fiercely*: I suppose you still want him.

ANNA : I don't want him any more. I don't want to see him, hear him. But he's in me — that's a fact. I wouldn't do a thing to harm him.[84]

> *She takes the ticket and her papers and tears them into scraps.* MARTINS *watches her with gloomy acquiescence.*

ANNA : I loved him. You loved him, and what good have we done him? Oh love! Look at yourself in the window — they have a name for faces like that . . .[85] [informers.

> MARTINS *stares into the window of the compartment.*

MARTINS : You talk too much.

> *A long silence follows. When he turns his head again*

---

[83] In the film, the dialogue runs:
MARTINS : Anna, don't you recognise a good turn when you see one?
ANNA: You have seen Calloway. What are you two doing?
MARTINS *angrily, his nerves breaking*: They want me to help take him.
ANNA: Poor Harry.
MARTINS: Poor Harry? Poor Harry wouldn't even lift a finger to help you.

[84] In the film, MARTINS adds here: 'Oh, Anna, why do we always have to quarrel?' The train pulls out past the buffet window, as ANNA replies: 'If you want to sell yourself, I'm not willing to be the price.'

[85] In the film, the scene ends with ANNA leaving the buffet, and MARTINS staring at the swinging door, while his coat lies discarded on the floor.

she has gone. His coat lies at his feet. As he stoops to pick it up, the train begins to pull out. Dissolve.]

121. CALLOWAY'S OFFICE (NIGHT):

Calloway and Martins together. Calloway stands with his back to Martins and his eyes on the map of Vienna.

Martins : I want to catch the first plane out of here.

Calloway : So she talked you round?

Martins *holding out the scraps of paper* : She gave me these.

Calloway *sourly* : A girl of spirit.

Martins : She's right. It's none of my business.

Calloway : It won't make any difference in the long run. I shall get him.

Martins : I won't have helped.

Calloway : That will be a fine boast to make [to your children.] *He puts his finger on the map as though he is still planning Lime's capture. Then he shrugs and turns to Martins.* Oh, well, I always wanted you to catch that plane, didn't I?

Martins : You all did.

Calloway *going to the telephone* : I'd better see if anyone's at the terminus still. You may need a priority.

Dissolve.

122. CALLOWAY'S CAR : BACK PROJECTION (NIGHT):

Paine is driving. Calloway is sitting in silence, Martins beside him.

Calloway : Mind if I drop off somewhere on the way? I've got an appointment. Won't take five minutes.

Martins nods. They draw up outside a large public building.

Calloway : Why don't you come in too! You're a writer : it should interest you.

Dissolve.

123. CHILDREN'S HOSPITAL (NIGHT):

As they come through the doors, a Nurse passes and Martins realises he has been shanghai-ed, but it is too late to do anything.

[Calloway : I want to take a look in No. 3 Ward.

NURSE : That's all right, Colonel Calloway.

CALLOWAY *to* MARTINS : You've been in on this story so much, you ought to see the end of it.]

124. CHILDREN'S WARD (NIGHT):

He pushes open a door and, with a friendly hand, propels MARTINS *down the ward, talking as he goes in a cheerful, professional, apparently heartless way. We take a rapid view of the six small beds, but we do not see the occupants, only the effect of horror on* MARTINS'S *face.*

CALLOWAY : This is the biggest children's hospital in Vienna [— very efficient place. In this ward we have six examples — you can't really call them children now, can you? — of the use of the Lime penicillin in meningitis . . . Here in this bed is a particularly fascinating — example, if you are interested in the medical history of morons . . now here . . .

MARTINS *has seen as much as he can stand.*

MARTINS : For pete's sake, stop talking. Will you do me a favour and turn it off?][86]

As they continue their walk past the small beds, dissolve.

125. CALLOWAY'S CAR : BACK PROJECTION (NIGHT):

They are driving together again in CALLOWAY'S *car.* MARTINS *is not speaking.*

CALLOWAY : For a good read I like a Western. Paine's lent me several of your books. ' The Lone Rider ' seemed a bit drawn out — you don't mind my talking frankly, do you? But I thought the plot of ' Dead Man's Ranch ' was pretty good. You certainly know how to tell an exciting story.

MARTINS *sullenly* : All right, Callaghan, you win.

CALLOWAY : I didn't know they had snake charmers in Texas.

MARTINS : I said you win.

CALLOWAY : Win what?

---

[86] In the film, the scene runs:

CALLOWAY : . . . All the kids in here are the results of Lime's penicillin racket . . .

He and MARTINS *inspect the beds.* MARTINS'S *face is full of anxiety and compassion, as* CALLOWAY *indicates a particular child's bed.*

CALLOWAY, *off-handedly* : Had meningitis . . . Gave it some of Lime's penicillin. Awful pity, isn't it?

MARTINS : I'll be your dumb decoy duck.

Dissolve.

126. CAFE (NIGHT):

A thin drizzling rain falls and the windows of the café continually cloud with steam. MARTINS sits gloomily, drinking cup after cup of coffee, and the clock in the café points to a quarter past midnight. There are only two other people in the café. Once, as somebody opens the door of the café, we see MARTINS put a hand to his pocket and we are aware that he has a revolver there.

127. CAFE STREET. LOCATION (NIGHT):

Outside the café preparations are being made for HARRY'S capture; the kiosk and the empty rain-wet street, and then at discreet intervals, well away from the scene, groups of POLICE.

128. SQUARE (WITH MANHOLE IN DISTANCE). LOCATION (NIGHT):

Last, under the trees of a square, sheltering as well as they can from the rain, CALLOWAY, PAINE and a group of SEWER POLICE; men with peaked caps, rather like lumberjacks, with big thigh-length boots; one man has a small searchlight hung on his chest; all carry revolvers. A manhole in the square is ready open.[87]

[129. TELEPHONE BOX. LOCATION (NIGHT):

---

[87] In the film, the scene continues:

A huge shadow looms against a house front near the café. PAINE, CALLOWAY and the soldiers stiffen and signal to each other. An aged BALLOON-SELLER shuffles into shot. While they are distracted, ANNA dives into the café.

PAINE : Look sir!

CAFE (NIGHT):

In the café, ANNA sits down and asks MARTINS:

ANNA : How much longer are you going to sit here?

CAFE SQUARE (NIGHT):

Return to the waiting men:

PAINE : Shall I go over there, sir?

CALLOWAY : No, leave them for a while.

The BALLOON-SELLER shuffles and sways towards CALLOWAY and PAINE, who try to sink into the shadows. But the old man pesters them until PAINE rapidly makes a purchase to get him out of the way.

A telephone begins to ring in a nearby box, and CALLOWAY *answers it. Only half of the conversation is heard, but we can gather* MARTINS *is on the other end.*

CALLOWAY: I told you to keep away from the telephone unless it was urgent. I don't care if you've drunk twenty cups. They'll help to keep you awake.

130. CAFE SQUARE. LOCATION (NIGHT):

He goes disgruntedly back to PAINE.

CALLOWAY: He's getting tired of it already, and he's only had two hours. Listen, Paine, get back to the office, slip on civvies, and go along to him. He'll be doing something foolish. Don't forget your gun.]

131. ROOF TOP. LOCATION (NIGHT):

We see HARRY *beside a chimney stack, silhouetted by bombed ruins against the sky, looking grimly down. From this angle, the square seems deserted. Then he turns and watches the window of the café.*

[MARTINS *returns to his table from the telephone.* HARRY *moves forward.*

132. CAFE (NIGHT):

MARTINS *to* WAITER: Coffee, more coffee.

The clock stands at 12:45. MARTINS *rubs the pane free from steam and peers out at the dreary empty street. Then he turns again and sips disconsolately at his coffee. He is divided in mind, between the sight he saw in the hospital of* HARRY'S *victims, and the consciousness of the role he is himself playing, of decoy to his friend. The door of the café creaks, and his hand again goes to his pocket. A girl in a wet mackintosh comes in. It is* ANNA.

MARTINS: So it's you.

ANNA: It's me. You can take your hand away.

She sits down at the table between him and the door, and he sheepishly withdraws his hand with a packet of cigarettes.

MARTINS: I was only looking for a cigarette.

ANNA: How much longer are you going to sit here?

MARTINS: Until I'm tired of it.

ANNA: Harry won't come. He's not a fool.

MARTINS: I wonder.

ANNA : What's your price this time?

MARTINS : No price, Anna.

ANNA : Honest, sensible, sober, harmless Rollo Martins. You are sober, aren't you?

MARTINS : They only serve coffee.

The door creaks again and he puts his hand to his pocket. He tries to see, but ANNA *is between him and the door.*

MARTINS : Get away.

ANNA : No.

But it is only an OLD WOMAN *selling bootlaces.*

MARTINS : I'll have you thrown out.

MARTINS *gets up and goes to the telephone behind the bar.* ANNA *follows him.* MARTINS *dials and waits with his eyes on* ANNA. *Unseen by both of them,* HARRY *suddenly appears — not through the main door, but by the back way. He grins when he sees* MARTINS *by the telephone.*

MARTINS : Is that Calloway? Listen. Anna's here. I can't get her to move.

They turn and see HARRY.

ANNA : Harry! Run, the police.

MARTINS *into the receiver* : He's here, Calloway.

HARRY *brings out his gun. (Still on page 53)*

ANNA : No, Harry . . . Run . . .

She is between HARRY *and* MARTINS, *and* HARRY *cannot shoot.* HARRY *wavers.* PAINE *is passing the window.* HARRY *lowers his gun and makes for the door.* MARTINS *drops the receiver and lets it dangle. He makes for the door, pushing* ANNA *on one side, but* HARRY *is already reaching the kiosk.* PAINE *at that moment reaches the café door.*][88]

---

[88] In the film, the scene in the café runs:

MARTINS: You should have gone. How did you know I was here, anyway?

ANNA: From Kurtz. They've just been arrested . . . But Harry won't come. He's not a fool.

MARTINS: I wonder.

CAFE SQUARE (NIGHT):

The POLICEMEN *wait. (Continued over.)*

[133. KIOSK STREET. LOCATION (NIGHT):
   PAINE *draws his gun, but it is too late. The kiosk is between them.*

PAINE : Why didn't you shoot, sir?
   They both begin to run down the street.

134. SQUARE WITH MANHOLE: LOCATION (NIGHT):
   CALLOWAY *drops the receiver back with impatience. Outside the telephone box he calls to the* SEWER POLICE *in German.*

CALLOWAY : Wir gehen hinunter. *He turns to a young British* OFFICER *who is with the party.* Carter, get all the manholes closed — he's gone down.][89]
   The party begin to file down the manhole.

135. WINDING IRON STAIRCASE FROM THE KIOSK: LOCATION (NIGHT).
   PAINE *goes first, shining a torch, and* MARTINS *follows.*

136. MANHOLES ON THE RIM OF THE CITY: LOCATION (NIGHT):

CALLOWAY : Yes, Paine, slip across and see what she's up to.
   PAINE *leaves.*

CAFE (NIGHT):
   ANNA *is speaking bitterly to* MARTINS.

ANNA : What's your price this time?
   The back door of the café opens.

MARTINS : No price, Anna.

ANNA : Honest, sensible, sober Holly Martins. Holly, what a silly name. You must feel very proud to be a police informer.
   HARRY *has entered quietly, (Still on page 54) overhears the word ' informer', and frowns.* ANNA *turns away from* MARTINS *and catches sight of* HARRY.

ANNA : Harry, get away, the police are outside!
   HARRY, *drawing his gun, signals* ANNA *out of the line of fire between himself and* MARTINS, *but* PAINE *is already making for the main door, so* HARRY *dashes out of the back door.*

[89] In the film, the following shots are seen:
THE RUINS OF VIENNA (NIGHT):
   HARRY *runs across bomb-sites, as the chase is raised with shrill whistles and shouts. Dogs bark and sirens hoot.*

A SQUARE (NIGHT):
   HARRY *clatters across a square to an open manhole and leaps in.* PAINE, CALLOWAY, MARTINS *and the* POLICEMAN *quickly catch up.* POLICEMAN *quickly catch up.*

114

[*The police are clamping them down.*]⁹⁰

137. THE SEWERS. LOCATION (NIGHT):

It is just past high tide when Martins *and* Paine *reach the river; first the curving iron staircase, then a short passage so low they have to stoop, and then the shallow edge of the water laps at their feet.* Paine *shines his torch along the edge of the current.*

[Paine : He's down here, sir.

Just as a deep stream when it shallows at the rim leaves an accumulation of debris, so the sewer leaves in the quiet water against the wall a scum of orange peel, old cigarette cartons and the like, and in this scum Harry Lime *has left his trail as unmistakably as if he had walked in mud.* Paine, *shining his torch ahead with his left hand, carries his gun in his right.*

Paine : Keep behind me, sir, he may shoot.

Martins : Why the devil should you be in front?

Paine : It's my job, sir. You're only a civilian.

The water comes halfway up their legs: Paine *keeps his torch pointing down and ahead at the disturbed trail at the sewer's edge. He takes a whistle out of his pocket and blows, and very far away there come the notes of the reply.*

Paine : They are all down here now. The sewer police, I mean. They know this place as I know the Tottenham Court Road. I wish my old woman could see me now.

He lifts his torch for a moment to shine it ahead, and at that moment a shot comes. The torch flies out of his hand and falls in the stream.

Paine : Nasty!

Martins : Are you hurt?

---

⁹⁰ In the film, there are the following scenes:
The Police *pour down every available manhole.*

THE SEWERS (NIGHT):
The Police *search, watch and shout in the echoing tunnels.*
They spot the fleeing Harry *several times (Still on page 103)*
Various shots of Harry *hiding on a gallery. (Still on page 104)*
Other shots of him hiding as the Police *pass. (Still on page 105)*

PAINE : Scraped my hand, sir, that's all. A week off work. Here, take this other torch, sir, while I tie my hand up. Don't shine it. He's in one of the side passages.

> *For a long time the sound of the shot goes on reverberating; when the last echo dies, a whistle blows ahead of them.* PAINE *blows an answer. He gives a low laugh in the darkness.*

PAINE : This isn't my usual beat. Do you know the ' Horseshoe ', sir?

MARTINS : Yes.

PAINE : And the ' Duke of Grafton '?

MARTINS : Yes.

PAINE : Well, it's a small world. The things you must have seen in Texas and those parts, sir. Me — I've led a very sheltered life. Careful, sir. It's slippery here. Fancy me being here with Rollo Martins.

MARTINS : Let me go first. I want to talk to him.

PAINE : I've orders to look after you, sir.

MARTINS : That's all right. I don't think he'll shoot at me.

> MARTINS *edges round* PAINE, *plunging a foot deeper in the stream as he goes. When he is in front, he calls out.*]

MARTINS : Harry.

> *The name sets up an echo, ' Harry, Harry, Harry ', that travels down the stream and wakes a whole chorus of whistles in the darkness. He calls again.*

MARTINS : Harry. Come out. It's no use.

> *A voice startlingly close makes them hug the wall.*

HARRY'S VOICE *off* : Is that you, old man? What do you want me to do?

MARTINS : Come out. And put your hands above your head.[91]

[HARRY'S VOICE : I haven't a torch, old man. I can't see a thing.

---

[91] In the film, the following sequence appears :

> PAINE *dashes out to warn* MARTINS.

> PAINE : Get back, get back, sir!

> PAINE *is standing right in the middle of the tunnel and does not realise where* HARRY *is hiding.* HARRY *shoots him down. The shot echoes round and round as* PAINE *subsides onto the cobbles.* CALLOWAY *strides out of the shadows and shoots* HARRY, *as the latter makes another break.* HARRY *falls, and scrambles away.*

MARTINS : Get flat against the wall. Harry, I'm going to shine the torch . . . Come out . . . You haven't got a chance.

He flashes the torch on, and twenty feet away at the edge of the light and the water, HARRY steps into view.

MARTINS : Hands above the head, Harry.

HARRY raises his hands and then, snatching his revolver from his breast pocket, fires with his left hand. The shot ricochets against the wall a foot from MARTINS'S head and he hears PAINE cry out. At the same moment a searchlight from fifty yards away lights the whole channel, catching HARRY in its beams. Next to MARTINS, the dead eyes of PAINE slumped at the water's edge with the sewage washing to his waist. An empty cigarette carton wedges into his armpit and stays. CALLOWAY'S party has reached the scene. MARTINS stands dithering above PAINE'S body, with HARRY LIME halfway between him and CALLOWAY. CALLOWAY'S party cannot shoot for fear of hitting MARTINS, and the light of the searchlight dazzles LIME.

CALLOWAY : Get back against the wall, Martins.

CALLOWAY'S lot move slowly on, their revolvers trained for a chance, and LIME turns this way and that way like a rabbit dazzled by headlights.

MARTINS *suddenly* : This way, Harry.

HARRY turns and runs past MARTINS, and the others cannot shoot. At the edge of the searchlight beam, he takes a flying leap into the deep central rushing stream, and the current carries him rapidly on into the dark.

CALLOWAY : Shoot, you fool, shoot.

MARTINS still dithers. CALLOWAY and his party fire blindly into the dark and a cry comes back to them.

CALLOWAY : Got him.

CALLOWAY and his men advance.

CALLOWAY *to* MARTINS *quite gently* : You didn't do him any good.

He halts by PAINE'S body. He is dead. His eyes remain blankly open as they turn the searchlight on him; somebody stoops and dislodges the carton and throws it in the river which whirls it on.

CALLOWAY: Poor old Paine. *He looks up and* MARTINS *has gone.* Martins! Martins! *His name is lost in a confusion of echoes, in the rush and roar of the underground river.*]

MARTINS *is wading upstream to find* HARRY. *He is afraid to lift the torch. He does not want to tempt him to shoot again.* HARRY *has been struck by the random bullets. He scrambles with difficulty out of the water, falls on his knees and begins to crawl up a side passage. He reaches the foot of the iron stairs. (Still on page 106) Thirty feet above his head is a manhole, but he would not have the strength to lift it, and even if he succeeded the police are waiting above. He knows all that, but he is in great pain, and cannot think rationally. He begins to pull himself up the stairs, but then the pain takes him and he cannot go on.* MARTINS *wades through the dark.*[92]

[MARTINS *calling not very loud*: Harry. *He turns back along the edge of the stream and finds his way up the passage which* HARRY *has taken.* Harry.

HARRY: Rollo.

MARTINS *puts his hand on an iron handrail and climbs only three steps up, his foot steps down on a hand, and there is* HARRY. MARTINS *shines his torch on him: he has not got a gun: he must have dropped it when the bullets hit him. For a moment* MARTINS *thinks he is dead, but then he whimpers with pain.* HARRY *swivels his eyes with a great effort to* MARTINS'S *face.*

CALLOWAY'S VOICE: Martins, where are you?

MARTINS: Here.

CALLOWAY'S VOICE: Don't take any chances, Martins. Shoot . . .

MARTINS *looks down and sees* HARRY *looking up at him.*

---

[92] In the film, this sequence continues:
A GRILLE AT STREET LEVEL (NIGHT):
  The wounded HARRY *reaches a grille at street level. His fingers clutch and claw at the heavy grating, unable to move it.*
THE SEWERS (NIGHT):
  MARTINS *follows* HARRY *up to the foot of the iron stairway and sees him struggling with the grille.* HARRY *is in great pain and fear.*

118

HARRY *winks.*] CALLOWAY *and his men reach the end
of the passage behind the searchlight. They hear a shot
and halt, turning on the light.* MARTINS *comes out into
the beams with hanging head. Dissolve.*

138. THE CENTRAL CEMETERY. LOCATION (DAY):
The coffin of HARRY LIME *is being lowered into the
grave, just as in the first sequence except that now only
three figures stand around the grave:* ANNA, MARTINS,
CALLOWAY. *But* KURTZ *and* TYLER *are missing.*

PRIEST: Anima ejus, et animae omnium fidelium defunctorum, per misericordiam Dei requiescant in pace.

ANNA: Amen.

The PRIEST, *again as in the previous sequence, takes a
spoon of earth and drops it onto the coffin. He hands the
spoon to* MARTINS *who does the same. This time* ANNA
*takes it, and she drops the earth too. Then, as before,
she walks away without a word.* MARTINS *and* CALLO-
WAY *walk together in silence towards the jeep, down one
of the long avenues.* [CALLOWAY *puts his hand on*
MARTINS'S *arm. It is almost the first real gesture of
friendship he has shown.*

CALLOWAY: Better dead.

MARTINS *reacts in just the opposite way as he reacted to*
ANNA *in the café.*][93]

MARTINS: A man's not dead because you put him underground.

We watch the worried reaction on CALLOWAY'S *face. He
glances over his shoulder towards the grave, remembering
only too well that the first time* HARRY LIME *was not
dead. They reach the car and climb in. There is no* PAINE
to drive them now. CALLOWAY *takes the wheel.*

139. CAR. BACK PROJECTION (DAY):
CALLOWAY *pushes at the starter.* MARTINS *is looking*

---

[93] In the film, the dialogue originally written for the following scene,
appears here:
CALLOWAY: What time do you make it?
MARTINS: Three-thirty.
CALLOWAY: We'll have to step on it, if you're going to catch that
plane.

ahead down the road towards the receding figure of ANNA.

MARTINS : What about Anna, Calloway?

CALLOWAY : I'll do what I can — if she'll let me.

They drive out of the cemetery. This time it is MARTINS *who looks out at* ANNA.

140. CEMETERY STREET . LOCATION (DAY):
ANNA *is on her way to the tram-stop, walking down the long dreary road.*

141. CAR : BACK PROJECTION (DAY):

MARTINS : Put me down a moment, Calloway.

CALLOWAY : There's not much time.

MARTINS : I can't just leave . . .

CALLOWAY *slows the car and brings it to a stop.*

142. CEMETERY STREET . LOCATION (DAY):

CALLOWAY : Be sensible, Martins.

MARTINS *as he stands beside the jeep* : I haven't got a sensible name . . . Callaghan.

He begins to walk down the road. CALLOWAY *turns and watches.* ANNA *is approaching.* MARTINS *stops and waits for her. (Still on page 106)* [*She reaches him and he seeks in vain for a word. He makes a gesture with his hand, and*] *she pays no attention, walking right past him and on into the distance.* MARTINS *follows her with his eyes.* [*From outside our vision we can hear a car horn blown again and again.*]

THE END

WATKINS COLLEGE OF ART
The third man: a film,
771.10 Gre

3928